PAUL & VIRGINIA

Jacques-Henri
BERNARDIN DE SAINT-PIERRE

PAUL & VIRGINIA

Translated from the French and with
an introduction by
John Donovan

Peter Owen
London and Chester Springs

PETER OWEN PUBLISHERS
73 Kenway Road, London SW5 0RE

Peter Owen books are distributed in the USA by
Dufour Editions Inc., Chester Springs, PA 19425-0007

This translation first published 1982
English translation, introduction and notes © John Donovan 1982
This paperback edition published 2005

ISBN 0 7206 1231 4

A catalogue record for this book is available from the British Library.

Printed and bound in Great Britain by Bookmarque Ltd, Croydon, Surrey

CONTENTS

ILLUSTRATIONS

1 The Childhood of Paul and Virginia.
   Engraving by Bourgeois de la Richardiere
   from a drawing by Lafitte

2 Crossing the Torrent.
   Engraving by B. Roger from a drawing
   by A. L. Girodet

3 The Bird's Nest.
   Engraving by O. Smith from a drawing
   by Tony Johannot and Français

4 Malabar Women Washing Virginia's Body.
   Engraving by T. Williams from a drawing
   by Tony Johannot

The four plates have been reproduced from the two most important of the many illustrated editions of *Paul and Virginia*. Plates 1 and 2 are taken from the edition of 1806 (printed by P. Didot), for which Bernardin had raised a subscription; 3 and 4 from the splendid *édition de luxe* published by L. Curmer in 1838.

The map of the Ile de France on page 36 has been redrawn after a manuscript map of the island done in ink and outlined in watercolour by Bernardin de Saint-Pierre himself. The original is in the Bibliothèque Municipale du Havre, where the majority of Bernardin's manuscripts are preserved. Some of the place-names are given in English, in accordance with the practice of the translation.

ACKNOWLEDGEMENTS

I am grateful to my colleagues R. T. Jones, who read and criticized the translation, and Nicole Ward-Jouve, who helped with the interpretation of some difficult passages. I should also like to thank Dan Franklin of Peter Owen Ltd for a most attentive reading of the manuscript and for many helpful suggestions.

University of York,   John Donovan
March 1982

To my mother

INTRODUCTION

Paul and Virginia claims a special place among serious European novels. First published in 1788 and an instant 'best-seller' of great popular appeal, it continued to enjoy the esteem of critics and – perhaps more remarkably – novelists of importance, for a century after its appearance. The story of the idyllic infancy and childhood of two children of French parentage on a tropical island, their growing love in adolescence, their separation and untimely deaths, its blend of exoticism and minute observation, of pastoral and tragic themes, has always made it difficult to classify. But if it has sometimes been regarded as a curiosity, it is nonetheless recognized as among the considerable achievements of the eighteenth-century novel in France, and it remains one of the notably successful attempts in Romantic literature to combine the extremes of a substantive criticism of life and a thoroughgoing naivety.

This 'manual of naive love'[1] has been through hundreds of editions in France and has been translated into the major European languages. In English alone, if we count collected and selected editions of Bernardin de Saint-Pierre's works as well as separate editions of the novel, figures of sixty printings before 1900 in England and twenty-five in America would seem to be fair, though probably conservative, estimates. (An *emigré*, returning to France from London where he had settled and become a bookseller, told Bernardin in 1803 that sales of *Paul and Virginia* alone had enabled him to live comfortably in exile.)[2] *Paul and Virginia* inspired songs and poems, plays, ballets, operas and musical entertainments. One of the most richly and variously illustrated of novels, it also provided the material for numerous sets of engravings and lithographs produced independently of the text, as well as paintings, theatrical posters and two silent films. Favourite scenes from the life of its hero and heroine regularly appeared on china, articles of clothing and miscellaneous decorative objects throughout the nineteenth century.[3]

References to the novel abound in nineteenth-century fiction. Incidents from *Paul and Virginia* decorate the walls of the Café de la Paix in Balzac's *The Peasants*. 'Well,' exclaims Vautrin in *Old Goriot*, as he discovers Rastignac asleep with his head on Victorine Taillefer's shoulder, 'here is a scene that would have provided the good Bernardin de Saint-Pierre, author of *Paul and Virginia*, with the inspiration for some beautiful passages.' The book appears in Flaubert's story 'November', in the hands of the prostitute Marie, who has read it a hundred times; and in the same author's 'A Simple Soul' Madame Aubin's son and daughter are victims of the sentimental fashion for naming children Paul and Virginia, after the famous pair whose names had become synonyms for chaste and exalted attachment in youth. Clarence Hervey, in Maria Edgeworth's *Belinda*, thinks fit, because of a fancied resemblance to Bernardin's heroine, to bestow the name of Virginia Saint-Pierre on the artless and uncorrupted girl he has discovered living with her grandmother in a cottage in the New Forest, and whom he decides to educate, like Sophie in Rousseau's *Emile*, to be his wife. In *Little Dorritt,* we are not surprised to hear Flora Finching remind Arthur Clennam of a youthful rebuff :

and you must be very well aware that there was Paul and Virginia which had to be returned and which was returned without note or comment;

though we may wonder that Phillotson, the schoolmaster in *Jude the Obscure*, is reminded by Jude and Sue 'of Paul and Virginia a little'. Its persistent presence in the literature of the age confirms the status of *Paul and Virginia* as one of those books which had established its own very particular place in the cultural life of the nineteenth century. It functioned, evidently, as a reference-point and imaginative node for ideas of primitivism, childhood love, natural education and sexual innocence, and, as such, exercised an unusually rich and varied influence on literary creation.

When *Paul and Virginia* was published in 1788, its author, Jacques-Henri Bernardin de Saint-Pierre, was fifty-one years old.[4] A native of Normandy and exceptionally widely travelled, he had been living in Paris since 1771. During this time he had sought in vain to secure employment with government ministries, whilst working at a number of literary projects which had been variously received. *Paul and Virginia* was not his first success; in 1784 his *Studies of Nature,* a series of moral and philosophical essays discovering the operation of Divine Providence in the beneficence of the natural world, had, against all expectation, found favour with a wide public, calling for a second edition, then a third. As if to ensure prosperity by association, he included his pastoral novel in the fourth volume of this edition. The success of the *Studies* brought an improvement in his financial position as well as a deluge of admiring letters, invitations, even offers of marriage; *Paul and Virginia* ensured him a regular income and made him both the object of a cult and a novelist of European reputation.

This abrupt turn in his fortunes came none too soon for a man whose existence had been a strenuous pursuit of recognition for rich and peculiar talents. Bernardin was born into a modest bourgeois family in Le Havre in 1737. Despite what he himself recognized as an obsessive personal ambition, his origins marked his opinions; he took decent independence and material frugality as an ideal of life and celebrated it in his writings. Private tradition traced noble descent on his father's side, a fiction that bolstered sagging family pride in difficult times and which Bernardin seems long to have entertained at some level of his mind, although he later admitted that the claim was without adequate foundation. From his mother he inherited the chronic nervous disability that affected a brother and sister as well as himself. As a child he was restive under correction at home and revolted by the harsh discipline of his religious masters at school. In old age, he recalled that the reading that most delighted and consoled him during these unhappy years was *Robinson Crusoe* and a folio volume of Saints' Lives.

At the age of twelve he was removed from school and sent with a sea-captain uncle on a voyage to Martinique from which he returned 'more disgusted with my uncle, with the vessel and with trade than with my teacher and his college'.[5] A major theme of his life had taken shape; all his future voyages were to end in disappointment. Having shown an aptitude for mathematics, in 1757 he entered the Ecole des Ponts et Chaussées in Paris to train as an engineer, but after less than two years French involvement in the Seven Years' War caused the school to be shut. Bernardin was appointed to a newly-formed corps of engineers and served under the Comte de Saint-Germain; he saw action with his regiment at Corbach and at Varbourg, but was ordered back to France after a quarrel with a superior officer. Almost immediately he was posted as engineer-geographer to Malta, which was then threatened with invasion by the Turks, but did not get on with his fellow engineers and returned in 1761 after a brief stay. For the next five years he pursued the uncertain career of a soldier of fortune in Holland, Russia, Poland and Germany. He had his share of reverses, as was inevitable without solid connections or influence; what is surprising is that he progressed as far as he did. But he was a young Frenchman of striking physical appearance and engaging disposition at a time when French language and culture were much admired east of the Rhine; he had some military training and experience, and he was prepared to go anywhere. Moreover he made friends easily and kept them for long years, many for life. He had intelligence, energy and resilience as well as occasional visitations of luck – the kind that seems to attend the true adventurer in need and, in his case, was perhaps nothing more than a penchant for creating the circumstances in which his gifts could operate with dramatic effect.

Certainly, his journeyings from court to court, mostly on very slender means, were not without their dramatic episodes. He entered the service of the Empress Catherine II of Russia as a lieutenant of engineers, but the extravagant projects brimming in his head – the formation of a company to find a passage through Russia to the Indies, the establishment of a republican community on the shores of Lake Aral – found no favour, and he left Russia in a mood of bitterness. A loan from a friend and a timely win at cards took him to Poland in June of 1764. Here he quickly involved himself in the rivalry and intrigues between the nationalist and Russian parties, first on one side, then on both. He frequented the circle of the Princess Marie Lubomirska,[6] with whom he was on terms of intimacy, and whose hospitality he enjoyed freely. For this robust and practised courtier, who had taken her first French lover when Bernardin was still a schoolboy, the 'Chevalier de Saint-Pierre' (as he now styled himself) conceived a passion that existed, according to his surviving papers, on several levels simultaneously, more or less fictionalized and romanticized. On his side it clearly fed on the need to dwell on the social distance between them, and to exaggerate it, and it lasted through a long correspondence where the physical distance was real enough. Marie had for some years made herself useful to the French secret service into whose employ Bernardin now entered with instructions to implant himself in the entourage of the new Polish king, Stanislas. But the king was unmoved by Bernardin's plan for raising fortifications along the Polish frontier and offered him only an artillery commission in a provincial garrison, which he considered beneath his capacities and which was certainly the death-blow to his aspirations in Poland. He determined to seek his fortune elsewhere and set out for Germany.

Thanks to the friendships he had made in Poland, and to letters from his secret service chief, he was able to give his address and quality in May 1765 as 'Monsieur de Saint-Pierre, Major and Aide de Camp to His Royal Highness the Elector of Saxony'. There must have been less than would seem to this office, for later in the summer he travelled to Berlin to offer his services at the court of Frederick II of Prussia. Success, if it was to be found anywhere, would surely be found here, where admiration for all things French, and especially French officers, was carried to the point of a mania. But the by now familiar pattern of high expectation, modest offer, indignant refusal, repeated itself, perhaps in this instance complicated by an ill-advised personal application to the king, and in the autumn of 1765 he was obliged to return to France.

In December his father died. In Normandy there were legal difficulties in settling the estate; Bernardin eventually sold his share and, back in Paris, moved into the first of a series of furnished lodgings. He now attempted to turn his recent experiences to advantage by presenting to the Foreign Minister his written observations on Holland, Russia and Poland, and to the Minister of War a *Mémoir on Desertion*. Whether the latter attracted attention or, what seems more likely, it was thought prudent to 'reward' an ambitious former agent who knew too much with an appointment far enough away to prevent him becoming an embarrassment,[7] Bernardin embarked in March 1768 on a mission to Madagascar as king's engineer with the rank of captain. He was soon on bad terms with the other members of the expedition and, to escape their animosity, he refused to disembark at Madagascar but continued with the ship to Mauritius, then a French colony : the Ile de France.

By this circuitous and unpredictable route, strewn with lost hopes and high-sounding titles, he reached the country that was to provide the setting and subject-matter of his masterpiece. At first he was unsure how to fill his time. His duties as king's engineer were not onerous, and such tasks as did come his way, like supervising the building of a bakery, could hardly engage the interest of one who had planned the fortifications of the Polish frontier. In his new situation his feelings were typically ambivalent; to his former patroness the Empress Catherine II he wrote :

> Here the countryside is without greenery, the walks without trees, the harbour without ships and trade without money. Finally, Madame, I know of hardly any place in the world better adapted to make a man a philosopher; in spite of oneself one grows accustomed to retirement, to abstinence and to all the virtues that attend on these conditions.[8]

To occupy his leisure he engaged in the usual trafficking in imported goods and this, together with his salary, enabled him to pay his debts, send money to family and friends and lay up a modest store against his return to France. To cure his loneliness he urged his attentions upon Madame Poivre, the wife of the island's administrator, persisting long after she had made it clear that she did not welcome them. Madame Poivre was a woman of sense and taste, in contrast to the white population in general, which revolted him by its ignorance, coarseness and dishonesty. 'They value nothing but double-dealing. When they want to indicate that a man is clever, they say he is cunning; but cunning is praise only for foxes.'[9]

Both circumstances and preference seemed to unfit him for the society of the island, but retirement sometimes takes on a more positive aspect than in the letter to Catherine II. He was consoled by seeing through the single window of the sparsely furnished log-cabin that served as his quarters :

> a profound solitude in which, despite the rocky landscape and the yellow grass, my imagination found repose. The remembrance of the friends I had left behind and my hopes of greatness troubled me, but . . . the beautiful sky and the steady murmur of the winds induced a state of gentle melancholy . . . full of charm and peace.[10]

Retirement and self-communion are regularly presented in Bernardin's writings as primary conditions of true knowledge of oneself and of nature. The soul in solitude, says the narrator of *Paul and Virginia*, becomes like a clear pool that reflects, 'together with its own banks, the greenery of the earth and the light of the heavens'. We may speculate with some confidence that it was solitude experienced in this way that revived his native energy and curiosity and directed them to the activity in which they were first to find significant expression – the exploration and description of natural things.

Around him lay an abundant and comparatively unexamined store, and he set about compiling a methodical catalogue of soil and rocks, trees and plants, animals, insects, shells and fishes. He made a journey into the interior of the island and another round the coastal districts, describing mountains, rivers and forests and correcting existing maps by his observations. He completed his general view – ' a countryside is the background to the portrait of human life'[11] – by considering the agriculture, commerce and defence of the island, and by reflections on the depravity of the white population and the brutal treatment of the slaves. Slavery as an institution he condemned as contrary to religion, humanity and politics. The arrival of a new governor unfriendly to Bernardin's interests and a new and hostile group of engineers made his departure a necessity. He accordingly embarked at Port Louis in November 1770 and, after a long and exhausting voyage, reached France at the end of May 1771. He had with him the manuscript of his travel-experiences, his financial situation was somewhat improved and he could look on his prospects with refreshed expectation.

Before long he was again making the soul-deadening rounds of the ministries. For the next thirteen years he never ceased to court the goodwill of the influential, seeking favours, support for commercial expeditions to the Indies and to America, gratifications, and recompense for his services in Poland. These efforts brought some results but they were notably slender and, after his earlier disappointments, left him with that distrust of the great which marks so much of his work and for which he had more cause than most. The publication in 1773 of the *Voyage à l'Ile de France*, his observations and description of the island to which he had added a journal of the outward and return voyages as well as various nautical and meteorological details, brought little reward. It had only a limited success with the public and received no official recognition. On his return to France, he had made the acquaintance of Rousseau, then living out his last years in Paris, and he maintained an intimate friendship with him until his death in 1778. The notes of their conversations, which he recorded, were meant to serve as the basis of a book defending the great man, with whose ideas he was largely, though not entirely, in agreement. (Bernardin never put the notes into the final form that he intended : they were published posthumously from his papers.)[12] After 1780 his energies were chiefly taken up with the composition of his major intellectual labour, *Studies of Nature*, a series of discourses in natural history and philosophy minutely illustrating a single leading idea : that in order to understand Nature aright one must recognize her beneficence, which is nothing other than the manifestation of Divine Providence. To pay the printer (no publisher would take the risk) he was obliged to appeal yet again to friends and patrons. *Studies of Nature* appeared in December 1784. The next year he was a writer of reputation and, thanks to the income from sales, official gifts and a pension, moderately well-off. Three years later, after the publication of *Paul and Virginia* in the third edition of the *Studies*, fame came at last and in a measure to satisfy even his ample and long-deprived appetite.

The first separate edition of the novel appeared in 1789; it sold spectacularly. Thereafter authentic and pirated editions multiplied. The small house Bernardin had bought in a modest quarter of Paris was deluged with letters praising the novelty of his descriptions, the purity of the affections he had rendered, the reality of his characters and, above all, the vivacity of the emotions he inspired. '*Paul and Virginia*,' wrote a priest from Gascony, 'has made all the world weep.'[13] He was hailed for standing against the current of a world-weary time by re-establishing in his book the old link between virtue and love, and for the sublimity of his moral teaching. For many, in an age that knew an upsurge in the cult of idealized Nature,[14] it provided both an intelligible key to her works and a guide for emotional response to them. It also supplied the text for a social ritual of the sensibilities. An anonymous letter from a priest living near Lyon recounts how he has read *Paul and Virginia* four times with a group of friends in sight of a meadow that recalled the valley on the Ile de France, and 'each time our cheeks were bathed in tears'.[15]

Among those who tasted to the full the melancholy pleasures of reading *Paul and Virginia* with a refined abandonment was Julie, Baronne de Krüdener, who later achieved fame as a Pietist, religious confidante of the Tsar Alexander I and proponent of the Holy Alliance. Madame de Krüdener lived in France from the summer of

1789 until the autumn of 1791, although she was then married to the Russian ambassador at Copenhagen. In Paris she met Bernardin, whom she was happy to acknowledge as both artist-philosopher and soul-mate, and kept up a long correspondence with him during her travels about the country.[16] From the Pyrenees in July 1790, where she has been marvelling at the awesome mountain scenery, she writes of savouring the rural tranquillity and the innocence of the country-folk, while dining on butter and black bread in a humble cabin and pouring out her gratitude to the divine goodness in a gush of tears before the altar of the village church. Into such surroundings bring a few like-minded friends with tender hearts and the scene is perfectly laid for the exhibition of Bernardin's gifts :

> Yesterday, on a high mountain, near a cabin that I love because the good woman who lives there makes maize-flour cakes for me, under some charming trees, I was with a young and engaging woman. She did not know *Paul and Virginia*. A man of high intelligence, preternatural imagination and comprehensive temperament was with us. He had been waiting a long time for *Studies of Nature* and was not yet acquainted with them. So I read *Paul and Virginia* aloud. Ah! you have no need of praise, but you could not have remained indifferent before that ascendancy, before that power with which your genius mastered these far from common souls, the exclamations that rendered homage to you, the tears that flowed from every eye. I have read *Paul and Virginia* many times myself, but I shed tears nonetheless and at the place where Paul has his last conversation with her, at the moment of departure, my voice was choked with emotion and weeping, and I had to leave off. We passed a delicious morning in this way and promised each other that we would return.[17]

When some allowance is made for aristocratic condescension, the intensity of Julie de Krüdener's response to *Paul and Virginia* and the high praise she reserves for its author are no doubt typical of sophisticated and cosmopolitan opinion among Bernardin's admirers, at any rate those who were prepared to lay themselves open to the full effect of his powers. She stands apart from them as the author of an unfinished and unpublished novel, 'The Cabin of the Latania-Trees',[18] in which the heroine's mind and heart have been formed by repeated readings of *Paul and Virginia*, thus creating an early example of a type of character that was to interest a number of later and greater writers. Such fictional exploration of the effects of a seminal novel on the minds of contemporaries is at once more searching and more difficult to estimate adequately than either personal testimony or discursive criticism; for here the means of investigation are the processes of fiction itself and the subject and starting-point the existence of a book that provides a rich new image of experience whose possibilities are tested and in a manner realized by new fictions.

George Sand's claim that she wrote *The Master Mosaic-Workers* for her son as an antidote to the effects of his reading *Paul and Virginia*[19] broadly defines the territory to be explored, the morbid consequences of exposure to a fiction that is both idealizing and catastrophic. This local and particular eruption of an old and deeply-rooted uneasiness about certain sorts of artistic representation – which Monsieur Etiemble's remark in the Preface to his 1965 edition of *Paul and Virginia* ('fodder unwisely offered to so many girls')[20] may be considered as prolonging into our own day – focused on Bernardin's novel for two generations after it appeared, and is in one sense the counter-movement to the opinion that made of it the literary monument of virtuous love. Lamartine's *Graziella*, Balzac's *The Village Priest* and Flaubert's *Madame Bovary* all introduce their heroines as if they were subjects of an experiment in psychology : more or less daughters of nature, having minds uninfluenced by romantic fiction before the first exposure in the form of *Paul and Virginia*. But the manifold hazards of the woman contemplating her own image is in each instance for the novelist much less a conclusion to be arrived at by analysis than a point of departure in the search for a new synthesis; and this impulse requires the reflexive method of turning the elements of the original fiction upon themselves. What if Virginia herself were to read *Paul and Virginia*?

Lamartine's Graziella, dark-eyed and pubescent, the daughter of simple Italian fisher-folk, finds herself sheltering from a spell of foul weather on an island in the Bay of Naples together with two French students among whose possessions is a copy of *Paul and Virginia*, that 'book which seems like a page of the world's childhood torn from the history of the human heart'.[21] One of the students translates the story aloud into Italian for the family on two successive evenings. Graziella is thunderstruck. 'The girl felt her soul, asleep till then, revealed to her in Virginia's soul. She seemed to have matured six years in that half hour. The stormy hues of passion mottled her forehead. . . .'[22] Such a concentrated dose of essential passion marks the beginning of grief for Graziella, but the students too are moved and troubled : 'The ravishing image of Graziella, transfigured by her tears, initiated into sorrow by love, floated through our dreams with the celestial creation of Virginia.'[23] Graziella eventually dies of her sorrowful passion. The fair image overpowers the dark one; the celestial virgin brings the experience of hell to the earthly maiden. Véronique Sauviat has a similar experience in Balzac's *The Village Priest*. She has known only pious books when at the age of eighteen she happens on *Paul and Virginia* on a bookstall and sits up all night to read it. 'A hand, should we say divine or diabolical, lifted the veil which had until then concealed Nature from her. . . . She was led by the mild and noble figure of the author towards that fatal human religion, the cult of the Ideal.'[24] This experience corresponds in the life of her affections to an attack of smallpox in her physical life; henceforward she is as damaged as the statue of the Virgin, mutilated during the Revolution, which stands outside her house and which her devout and avaricious parents keep supplied with the flowers that now seem to her more beautiful than they were and whose symbolic language she can hear for the first time.

Emma Bovary is already married and beginning to wonder how it is that love has not brought the happiness she had thought to be its natural condition when we are allowed our first glimpse into the formation of her mind :

> She had read *Paul and Virginia* and she had dreamed of the little bamboo house, the negro Domingue, the dog Fidele, but above all the sweet affection of some good little brother, who goes to fetch red fruit for you up in trees that are higher than church steeples, or who comes running barefoot across the sand bringing you a bird's nest.[25]

In thus rendering the primary matter of his heroine's imaginative life, Flaubert is more restrained and more precise than either of his predecessors, and as such the passage is an image of his admiration for Bernardin de Saint-Pierre. He enlarges upon this very pointedly in a letter written to Louise Colet during the composition of *Madame Bovary* :

> I think, contrary to your opinion this morning, that all subjects

can be made interesting. As for creating Beauty with them, I think so too, theoretically at least, but I am less sure. Virginia's death is very beautiful, but so many other deaths are equally moving (because Virginia's is exceptional)! What is *admirable* is the letter she writes to Paul from Paris. It always tears out my heart when I read it. There will be less weeping at the death of my old Bovary than at Virginia's, I am sure of that in advance.[26]

If it is interesting that he had the example of Virginia before him as he wrote, it may surprise that he establishes a connection between Virginia's death, abstracted from all but symbolic motifs like a saint's legend, and Emma's, where the proliferation of physical detail suggests the medical textbook. But the terms of his reflections define the grounds of similarity. This is not a matter of emotion; he is intent on creating beauty and has fixed his attention on the point at which emotion and beauty diverge, which is also the point where Virginia's and Emma's deaths come together. The beauty that unites them may finally be an imponderable term, but it is here made to carry the insight that is shared in some degree by Lamartine and Balzac – that the link between purity and death is an aesthetic one.

Bernardin is now remembered principally as the author of a classic novel, but during the latter half of his life he enjoyed considerable renown as a naturalist and a philosopher. Such was his reputation – and such his skill at adapting to changing political conditions – that he was appointed by Louis XVI in 1792 as Superintendent of the Royal Botanical Gardens and Curator of Natural History Collections, and by the Convention in 1794 as Professor of Moral Science at the new Ecole Normale Supérieure.[27] Neither position lasted for very long; but he became a Member of the Institute in 1795 and kept his place, despite quarrels with atheist members, until he entered the French Academy in 1803. He became President of the Academy in 1807, a year after receiving the Legion of Honour under the Empire.[28] *Paul and Virginia* was therefore soon known as the work of a man of science who was also a moral teacher. Bernardin himself frequently stressed its character as a philosophic and didactic novel, on one occasion claiming that it contained the result of all his philosophy.[29] In his 1788 Preface he declared that he had intended it to illustrate a number of great truths, among them, 'that our happiness consists in living according to Nature and virtue'; and in the Preamble to the 1806 edition he describes his novel as 'a relaxation from my *Studies of Nature*, and the application that I made of its laws to the happiness of two unfortunate families'.[30]

A contemporary reader who was acquainted with Bernardin's views on nature and society would have been in no doubt that his friend Rousseau had contributed largely to them.[31] That nature is the source of happiness and well-being; that to live according to her laws is to find peace, health and virtue; that all knowledge has its source in nature and is properly and spontaneously perceived by sentiment rather than reason; that organized political society tends to corrupt its citizens and establish inequality among them; that education according to nature is the means by which man's innate qualities can be developed and true equality among men restored – these, in broad terms and allowing for minor differences, are the foundation-principles of both men's social and ethical thought, and it is easy to discern their presence in *Paul and Virginia*. But Bernardin was too independent a spirit to follow another man's doctrines without question. He assured his sister that he had not wholly accepted, but rather chosen judiciously among Rousseau's ideas and writings.[32] It was on religious matters that he diverged most significantly. He maintained that parents should tell their children of the existence of God from an early age, as they were then capable of feeling His existence and loving Him, rather than wait until the age of fifteen, as Rousseau had recommended in *Emile*.[33] The mode of operation of Divine Providence was another point of difference. When Rousseau, in his old age, told him that Providence cared for the species but neglected the individual, Bernardin defended particular Providence, the mainstay of his own system of nature, by comparing it to the air that surrounds every object on earth, as well as the globe itself.[34] Yet he remained firm in his quasi-religious admiration for the master whom he predicted, in the 1806 Preamble to *Paul and Virginia*, would one day be as revered as Plato and Lycurgus.[35] He was not a slavish disciple, but the frequency with which he cites Rousseau's views and his example as an artist effectively constitutes a claim to be his intellectual successor.

During the period of their friendship in the 1770s, subjects for literary and historical works were a regular topic of their conversations. One of those which Rousseau had considered treating himself, and which he urged the younger man to take up, was to portray 'a

society made happy by the laws of nature and virtue alone'.³⁶ It was
a project to appeal to Bernardin's literary ambitions as well as his
philosophical preoccupations. He expressed a desire to carry it out, if
time, circumstances and his health allowed, and in fact gave much
thought to what such a work might contain. But, apart from a plan
of the whole, he completed only the first book, which he published
in 1788 under the title of *l'Arcadie.* He gives a fuller account of its
inception in a note at the end of the third volume of the *Studies of
Nature* :

> Such sweet relations are to be found in the harmonies between the
> different ages of human life . . . that I am astonished that no one
> has given at least a portrait of a human society living thus in accord
> with all the needs of existence and the laws of nature. . . . I had
> intended, at the suggestion of J.-J. Rousseau, to develop this idea
> by writing the history of a people of Greece who are well known to
> the poets because they lived according to nature, but for that
> reason virtually ignored by our political writers.³⁷

Bernardin's plan shows that it was by locating an ideal republic in
Arcadia, the archetypal region of pastoral poetry and romance, that
he intended to bring literature to the aid of political philosophy.³⁸ It
was indeed an ambitious project, and an extravagant one, but it
shows, at least, the seriousness with which he invested the pastoral
idea.

One of the reasons why his *Arcadie* never became anything more
than an interesting false start must have been that the subject of 'a
society made happy by the laws of nature and virtue alone' proved
to be better suited to the narrower canvas of *Paul and Virginia.* By
reducing the scale of his portrait he could bring its fundamental
philosophical issues into sharper focus. Together with Rousseau,
Bernardin believed the family to be the necessary basis of all social
organization. 'Families', he once said, 'are little nations.'³⁹ He may
also have remembered that in the *Discourse on the Origin of Inequality* Rousseau had identified a small grouping of families living
in a loose association of mutual need, equally removed from brutish-
ness and refinement, as the state of society most in conformity with
man's nature and most conducive to happiness.⁴⁰ In the event, he
chose in *Paul and Virginia* to treat a social group that is no larger than
a family; and if there were philosophical reasons for his choice, there

were also artistic ones. 'I wished', he wrote in the 1788 Preface, 'to join to the beauty of Nature between the tropics the moral beauty of a little society.' It is his simplest statement of his aim to create an aesthetic whole of his twin ideals of natural and social harmony.

In the same Preface Bernardin speaks of his novel as 'a species of pastoral', and he normally refers to it as a 'pastoral' in his later writings.[41] The term had a special meaning in his day; by appropriating it he associates his 'little book' not only with the classical poets Theocritus and Virgil, but also with the latest literary type to claim descent from them, the pastoral novel, which reached the height of its fashion in France in the 1780s.[42] The two most celebrated practitioners of the genre were the Swiss-German Salomon Gessner, whose *Daphnis* (1754) had achieved a European vogue, and the Frenchman Jean-Pierre Claris de Florian, whose *Galatée* (1783) and *Estelle* (1787) continued the tradition in his own country with even greater success. (All three works were translated into English before the end of the eighteenth century.) Florian prefixed to *Estelle* an 'Essay on Pastoral' in which, speaking from the summit of his acknowledged pre-eminence as a pastoral novelist, he reflects on the history of the genre and establishes a code of practice for its most recent manifestation. His readers are instructed, the year before the appearance of *Paul and Virginia,* that the pastoral should compose a touching picture of rustic behaviour; that its subject should be chosen so as to present virtuous and sensitive characters capable of sacrificing the most ardent passion to duty, and finding pleasure in duty itself; that the brilliance of their virtue should be enlivened by the natural beauty of their surroundings; that their actions should illustrate the teachings of a sweet and pure morality, as necessary to the shepherd as to the prince.[43] The love between maid and swain should be 'as pure as the crystal of their fountains', for 'the loveliest shepherdess would lose all her charms if she lost her modesty'.[44] Moreover, 'No bucolic poet would dare – and rightly – take for his heroine a shepherdess beguiled by riches or greatness.'[45] As for the style :

it should combine the qualities of the novel, the eclogue and the poem. It should be simple, as befits a narrative; it should be naive, because the characters it speaks of and allows to speak have no other eloquence than the eloquence of the heart; and it should be noble, because everywhere it treats of virtue; and virtue is always expressed nobly.[46]

The degree to which Bernardin's practice in *Paul and Virginia* con-
forms, in matter and method, to Florian's literary doctrines is clear
enough. His novel, which must have been all but finished by the end
of 1787 when *Estelle* appeared, can hardly owe a direct debt of any
substance to the 'Essay on Pastoral'; but like *Estelle*, which also tells
the story of two children of nature brought up in a mountain valley,
it worked a vein which was pretty well defined by the end of the 1780s.

The intellectual climate and literary fashion of the age thus com-
bined to create both the conditions from which *Paul and Virginia*
developed and the philosophical awareness and state of taste that
ensured its vogue. But when due allowance is made for these conditions, much remains to be considered; for, unlike other novels
popular in their day, it has survived the phase of thought and sensibility in which it was written to become a classic. As such, it claims
an interest beyond that of a happy experiment in a forgotten genre.
If, as Professor Jean Fabre suggests, the originality of *Paul and
Virginia* consists in being the perfection of the pastoral novel and, at
the same time, its contradiction,[47] then this is only partly accounted
for by saying that Bernardin did supremely well what others had
done before him. We must also recognize his determination to do
what others had neglected, to accommodate within a refined and
idealized literary form a sense of natural and social evil, and to express
both in terms of religious myth. Thus, the earthly paradise is
imagined as an outpost of empire into which political and social
prejudice finally penetrate to expel the inhabitants. The original sin
that Madame de la Tour and Marguerite commit is conceived of as
an offence against the marriage-code of a corrupt society. The virtue
that provides the motive for Virginia's self-martyrdom in the hurricane is modesty, which Rousseau had declared to spring from contact
with evil: 'Whoever blushes is already guilty; true innocence is
ashamed of nothing.'[48] The integrity of Bernardin's art is nowhere
more evident than in the prominence he gives to Virginia's death. In
so doing, he makes the cardinal point of his fiction an event which is
equally discordant to providential optimism and pastoral harmony,
and which strained the conventions of his chosen genre to their limits,
and beyond.

In one of his affirmations of realist faith Balzac maintained that the longevity of a work of fiction was a function of its veracity, of its relation to observed facts taken from actual life, and that novels which enjoyed prolonged success, like *Paul and Virginia*, were 'auto-biographical studies, or narratives of events sunk beneath the ocean of the world and recovered by the harpoon of genius'.[49] The metaphor is fitting for a story that ends in shipwreck, and the formula is remarkably apt for a novel in which a high proportion of incidents and places derive closely from observation and personal experience. The extent and importance of this debt to the actual will be appreciated if we return to Bernardin's stay on the Ile de France between 1768 and 1770 in order to look more closely at the circumstances and events that provided the material for his fiction.

Sometime during this period, and probably not long after his arrival, he learned of the tragic loss a quarter of a century earlier of the vessel the *Saint-Géran* within sight of the north-east coast of the island. The *Saint-Géran*, with 217 persons on board, sighted the Ile de France late in the afternoon of 17 August, 1744, after a five-month voyage from France. As the sea was calm and as illness, chiefly scurvy, had incapacitated many of the passengers and crew, leaving few fit enough to help with the manoeuvres necessary to come into port and drop anchor, the captain and officers decided to give them a night of rest by lying outside the harbour until morning. During the night the ship was carried by the currents round to the north-east of the island, where she ran onto a reef and broke up under the pounding of the waves near the Ile d'Ambre, with the loss of all but nine of those on board. No one witnessed the wreck from the shore, but a week later the survivors made depositions which establish some facts of first importance for *Paul and Virginia*.[50] There was no hurricane; this was Bernardin's invention. The passengers and crew were faced with the choice between remaining on board a ship that was listing and would soon sink, or taking their chances in a sea where the breakers and rocks were a deadly hazard. Two incidents stand out. Edme Caret, one of the survivors, fitted a plank with ropes at either end for himself and the captain, Monsieur Delamare, to float on, then suggested to the captain that he might save himself more easily if he removed his jacket and breeches. Monsieur Delamare replied in an access of heroic dignity and professional conscience 'that it would ill become the decency of his position to arrive on shore naked, and that he had papers in his pocket that he must not leave'.[51] Two other survivors who, fearing a squall, had leapt into the sea with a plank,

declared that at the moment of quitting the ship they had noticed
the situation of two women passengers : Mademoiselle Mallet on the
quarter deck with the second lieutenant, and Mademoiselle Caillou
on the forecastle with three other passengers and the first ensign,
Monsieur Longchamps de Montendre, who came down 'to throw
himself into the sea and almost immediately went up again to per-
suade Mademoiselle Caillou to save herself'.[52]

Here, clearly, are the elements of Bernardin's denouement, which
he has curiously transposed to form Virginia's death-scene. How did
he learn of the disaster? Not, it would seem, from the official documents which were discovered in the archives of the appeal court on
Réunion and published only in 1822,[53] and which had probably
been there since long before his arrival on the island. In all likelihood
he heard of it by word of mouth. Twenty-five years is well within the
span of living memory, and the account or accounts he was given may
have been full and accurate; but it is also long enough for an event of
outstanding local interest – and one which touches the lifeline of an
island colony – to change its shape and become embellished with
touches of fancy. That this is indeed what happened in the case of
the *Saint-Géran* is borne out by the reminiscences of one Madame
Journel,[54] who had been a settler on the Ile de France in the eighteenth century and had known the brother of the Mademoiselle
Caillou who perished in the wreck. Most of Madame Journel's memories are so manifestly influenced by recollections of the novel as to
be virtually disqualified as serious evidence; but by this very fact the
one important detail in her story that is not contained in the novel
assumes an air of authenticity : that during the voyage Mademoiselle
Caillou, who had been sent to complete her education in France, fell
in love with the ensign Longchamps de Montendre and that they
decided to marry on reaching the Ile de France.

Bernardin may have been told of this shipboard romance frustrated
by natural catastrophe; whatever he heard was likely to have been
wrought into romantic configuration, and 'the voice of the people',
which he imagines as taking up the tale of the wreck on the last page
of the novel, was probably responsible for the first steps towards the
fiction of *Paul and Virginia*. To this he joined the story of the two
families living a frugal and retired existence in a mountain valley
inland of Port Louis. In his 1788 Preface he affirms that his story 'is
true so far as its principal events are concerned', and that he has
added only a few insignificant details. This allows him a clear, if

modest, margin of invention which in the Foreword to the 1789 edition[55] has increased. Here he insists on the accuracy with which he has described places and manners and on the truth of the final catastrophe, but no longer on that of the principal events. He even goes so far as to caution against too minute an inspection of the reality behind the fiction by an analogy with the danger of destroying the rose's mystery by pulling apart its petals. A disingenuous warning, perhaps, in view of his earlier guarantee of authenticity, but a pretty sure indication that invention plays a larger role in the earlier parts of the story than the later.

Invention with him is often in its first stage a matter of selection and re-combination. The episode of the runaway slave is an interesting example of this process. In the *Voyage à l'Ile de France* Bernardin records how one day a female slave threw herself at his feet.[56] She feared the wrath of a cruel mistress whom she had displeased and begged him to ask for her pardon, which he obtained. Another time, having accepted an invitation to travel by dug-out canoe to visit a settler in the valley of the Black River, he decided to return on foot to Port Louis by way of the Williams Plains, armed with a brace of pistols against the danger from bands of runaway slaves. The journey was arduous and fraught with obstacles. He had to be carried across the rocky bed of a river on the shoulders of a slave; at sunset his guide lost his way in the thick woods at the foot of the Three Paps; and only after an exhausting night-trek did they encounter some black shepherds, one of whom led him to a nearby settlement.[57] Conflating the two actual incidents into a single fictional one, Bernardin incorporated practically every detail of any significance in his own accounts : lighting a fire by the friction of two sticks, discovering a stream with cress growing on its banks, shouting in the hopes of bringing help or at least rousing a dog, walking through the dark forest by torchlight; even Virginia's wounded feet are borrowed from an accident he had on another journey.[58] All this he suffuses with his own distress and anxiety, especially the fear of runaway slaves who, made desperate enough to escape the atrocious conditions of their servitude, were notoriously hostile to white travellers. But he goes beyond a reshuffling of his own adventures to add another dimension, which also has its roots in his stay on the island; he makes this first important experience the children have away from their mothers an initiation into adult sexuality. Writing of the manners of the white inhabitants in the *Voyage*, he had remarked :

There are very few married people in the town. Those who are not
rich plead the mediocrity of their fortune; others say that they
want to settle in France; but the ease of finding concubines among
the black women is the real reason.[59]

The black woman is thus associated with an illicit sexuality and
a threat to the ideal of the family, and something of this is carried
over to the slave of *Paul and Virginia*. Appearing suddenly one morning, she precipitates an adventure that is not without its innocent
eroticism (the walk arm in arm alone through the forest, the crossing
of the river), but with its cowed slave and trembling girl, its profane
and threatening man, its pipe and cane, belling stags and bleeding
feet, it is overshadowed by sexual menace. Paul, soon after he and
Virginia have retreated in dread, begins retrospectively to romanti-
cize his actions : he would have fought with the planter if he had
refused his pardon; later, in the love-songs they address to one
another, each recalls the journey to the Black River in lyrical terms
as marking an epoch in their lives. It has entered their personal mythology; they have taken the first steps towards accommodating the
unknown force. But circumstances prevent them from going further,
and the force escapes their control, only to combine with the other
forces at work which finally gather to destroy them.

The black slave-woman, clothed in a strip of rag and pursued
through the forest by white men and their dogs, stands at the utter
extreme from the white Virginia in her home, with her fair hair and
blue hood, who is found by a friendly dog when she is lost, and this
function is generalized to the other slaves. They are made to embody
the sexual powers that need to be excluded from the society of the
two families so long as their precarious idyll lasts. Virility, a force so
obviously destructive that every encounter with a man of virile age –
planter, priest, governor, naked sailor – is a movement towards
disaster, is safely domesticated only in the person of Domingue and
the friendly slave band that carries the children home. The slave-
woman, image of the desecrated female, carries the burden of
Virginia's sexuality, just as that of Madame de la Tour and Marguerite, which had been effectively spiritualized, makes its ghastly
re-emergence in the form of the Malabar women who prepare
Virginia's corpse for burial after her death.

The artful construction and resonant symbolism of the episode of the runaway slave was achieved, like the rest of *Paul and Virginia*, only after much hesitation, labour and revision. Tradition has it that Bernardin recopied the novel seven or eight times in his own hand.[60] However that may be, the only manuscript of any substance[61] known to survive, itself scribbled over with corrections and far from finished, represents an intermediate state between earlier drafts and the fair copy he must have made for the first edition of 1788. It seems to date from the period 1777-80. It is not known exactly what stages the novel passed through before and after that time, but the evidence of the manuscript itself suggests a long and painful gestation. At one point Bernardin envisaged adding to a new edition of the *Voyage à l'Ile de France*[62] an *Histoire de Melle Virginie de la Tour*, which is the title of the manuscript. He may have begun to make plans or sketches for this soon after his return to France or even while still on the island, and a period of composition extending over fifteen years is likely to be not far from the truth. Throughout this long process he shaped his materials – topographical, botanical, autobiographical, historical – into fiction under the imaginative pressure of his vision of universal struggle in the natural world, which is tempered by virtue and mysteriously directed by Divine Providence towards a state of ultimate harmony and perfect happiness. He elaborated this conception through the master-image of his characters' existence on a paradisal island enclosed in a destructive element.

Planned as part of a book of travel and geography and finally published at the end of a work of natural philosophy, *Paul and Virginia* shows both the scientist's concern for ordered detail and the speculative range of the philosopher. But what controls both is the artist's habit of exploring experience by metaphor and symbol. In the first paragraph the major elements of nature and civilization, which the families manage for a while to keep in a state of vital tension, are identified and placed in a symbolic landscape : the ruined cabins and fallow fields in the comforting enclosure of the valley; the forest, town, church and (especially) the sea from which danger comes in spite of all efforts to keep it away; the doom-laden titles of the places of suffering, Tomb Bay, the Cape of Misfortune; and the Coin de Mire standing like a temporary bastion against the ocean, where Virginia's death will bring all symbols together in the event that creates the harsh and impersonal beauty that Flaubert recognized.

For all that precedes the final catastrophe, the old man's attempt to console Paul provides the key metaphor :

If we, who owe nothing we have to ourselves, dared assign bounds
to the Power that has given us everything, might we not imagine
ourselves here as at the limits of His empire, where life struggles
with death and innocence with tyranny?

Everywhere the struggle is presented in terms that stress its cosmic
significance, its status as a principle of existence. Vegetables and
minerals are opposed as primal representatives of vitality and mor-
bidity. Crops and ornamental plants overcome the aridity of the
rocky valley; Paul makes pyramids of stone burst into flower, the
mountainside is covered with a curtain of greenery, aloes rise from
the rocks and reach out to flower-laden creepers. But the opposite
tendency has its own icy power : waves become architectural scrolls,
trunks of trees columns of bronze, falling water a sheet of crystal, and
the children themselves a marble statue of Niobe's children, who were
punished for their mother's sin. Against the work of the sculptor,
preferred by kings for its illusion of permanence, is set that of the
gardener and, most pertinently, the simple gardener Virginia, whose
papaw-tree will by natural generation outlive the monuments of
ambition. And opposed to the sculptor and the architect is the story-
teller, whose art lives in the succession of men like the gardener's art
in the succession of trees. He can articulate the significance of obscure
events, compose the inscription for the humble ruins with which the
story begins and ends, modulate the tragedy into milder mood :

Ruins where nature struggles with the art of man inspire a gentle
melancholy;[63]

and give proof of how much the story of simple lives can reveal to
the feeling heart and the attentive mind.

J.D.

REFERENCES

[1] Lamartine, *Graziella*, ed. Jean des Cognets (Paris: Garnier, 1960), p. 48.

[2] *'Préambule'* to the 1806 edition of *Paul et Virginie*, in *Paul et Virginie*, ed. P. Trahard (Paris: Garnier, 1964), pp. 11-12.

[3] See Paul Toinet, *Paul et Virginie: Répertoire Bibliographique et Iconographique* (Paris: Maisonneuve et Larose, 1963).

[4] The principal sources for Bernardin de Saint-Pierre's life are L. Aimé-Martin, 'Essai sur la Vie et les Ouvrages de Bernardin de Saint-Pierre', in *Oeuvres Complètes de Jacques-Henri Bernardin de Saint-Pierre* (Paris: Méquignon-Marvis, 1818), pp. 1-271; F. Maury, *Etude sur la Vie et les Oeuvres de Bernardin de Saint-Pierre* (Paris: Hachette, 1892); M. Souriau, *Bernardin de Saint-Pierre d'après ses Manuscrits* (Paris: Société Française d'Imprimerie et de Librairie, 1905); and *Correspondance de Jacques-Henri Bernardin de Saint-Pierre*, ed. L. Aimé-Martin, 4 Vols. (Paris: Ladvocat, 1826).

[5] M. Souriau, *Bernardin de Saint-Pierre*, op. cit., p. 19.

[6] See Jean Fabre, *Stanislas-Auguste Poniatowski et l'Europe des Lumières*, Publication de la Faculté des Lettres de l'Université de Strasbourg (Paris: Société d'Edition: Les Belles Lettres, 1952), pp. 284-8.

[7] Jean Fabre, *'Paul et Virginie, pastorale'*, in *Lumières et Romantisme* (Paris: Klincksieck, 1963), p. 169.

[8] Cited in *Paul et Virginie*, ed. P. Trahard, op. cit., p. ix.

[9] *Voyage à l'Ile de France*, in *Oeuvres Complètes*, op. cit., Vol. I, p. 147.

[10] M. Souriau, *Bernardin de Saint-Pierre*, op. cit., p. 92.

[11] *'Préface'* to *Voyage à l'Ile de France*, op. cit., Vol. I, p. 1.

[12] See Bernardin de Saint-Pierre, *La Vie et les Ouvrages de Jean-Jacques Rousseau*, ed. Maurice Souriau (Paris: Cornély, 1907).

[13] M. Souriau, *Bernardin de Saint-Pierre*, op. cit., p. 245.

[14] See Pierre Trahard, *La Sensibilité Révolutionnaire* (Paris: Boivin, 1936), Chapter VI.

[15] M. Souriau, *Bernardin de Saint-Pierre*, op. cit., p. 245.

[16] Francis Ley, *Madame de Krüdener et son temps 1764-1824* (Paris: Plon, 1961), Chapter 3.

[17] Francis Ley, *Bernardin de Saint-Pierre, Madame de Staël, Chateaubriand, Benjamin Constant et Madame de Krüdener (d'après des documents inédits)* (Paris: Aubier, 1967), p. 79; *Madame de Krüdener*, op. cit., pp. 620-1.

[18] Francis Ley, *Bernardin de Saint-Pierre*, op. cit., p. 90; *Madame de Krüdener*, op. cit., p. 146.

[19] George Sand, *Les Maîtres Mosaïstes* (Paris, 1838), *'Notice'*.

[20] *Romanciers Français du XVIIIe Siècle*, Vol. II, Bibliothèque de la Pléiade (Paris: 1965), p. xxxv.

[21] *Graziella*, op. cit., p. 48.

[22] Ibid., p. 59.

[23] Ibid., p. 62.

[24] Honoré de Balzac, *Le Curé de Village*, in *La Comédie Humaine*, Vol. VIII, Bibliothèque de la Pléiade (Paris, 1949), pp. 549-50.

[25] Gustave Flaubert, *Madame Bovary*, ed. C. Gothot-Mersch (Paris: Garnier, 1971), p. 36.

[26] *Oeuvres Complètes de Gustave Flaubert: Correspondance – Troisième Série: 1852-54* (Paris, 1927), p. 344.

[27] M. Souriau, *Bernardin de Saint-Pierre*, op. cit., Chapters XV and XVIII.

[28] Ibid., Chapters XIX and XXII.

[29] Ibid., pp. 235-6.

[30] *Paul et Virginie*, ed. P. Trahard, op. cit., p. 4.

[31] Pierre Trahard, *Les Maîtres de la Sensibilité Française au XVIIIᵉ Siècle* (Paris: Boivin, 1933), Vol. IV, pp. 7-45.

[32] M. Souriau, *Bernardin de Saint-Pierre*, op. cit., p. 136.

[33] *La Vie et les Ouvrages de Jean-Jacques Rousseau*, op. cit., pp. 151-5.

[34] M. Souriau, *Bernardin de Saint-Pierre*, op. cit., pp. 136-7.

[35] *Paul et Virginie*, ed. P. Trahard, op. cit., p. 57.

[36] *La Vie et les Ouvrages de Jean-Jacques Rousseau*, op. cit., p. 175.

[37] *Oeuvres Complètes*, op. cit., Vol. V, pp. 389-90.

[38] M. Souriau, *Bernardin de Saint-Pierre*, op. cit., p. 211.

[39] *La Vie et les Ouvrages de Jean-Jacques Rousseau*, op. cit., p. 166.

[40] *Discours sur l'Origine et les Fondements de l'Inégalité parmi les Hommes*, in *Oeuvres Complètes*, Vol. III, Bibliothèque de la Pléiade (Paris, 1964), pp. 169-71.

[41] See, for example, *'Préambule'* in *Paul et Virginie*, ed. P. Trahard, op. cit., pp. 4, 5, 11, 12 and 28; and M. Souriau, *Bernardin de Saint-Pierre*, op. cit., pp. 236 and 239.

[42] Jean Fabre, *'Paul et Virginie*, pastorale', op. cit., pp. 185-99.

[43] 'Essai sur la Pastorale', in *Estelle, Roman Pastoral*, 2nd ed. (Paris, 1788), pp. 1-42.

[44] Ibid., p. 21.

[45] Ibid., p. 30.

[46] Ibid., p. 36.

[47] Jean Fabre, *'Paul et Virginie*, pastorale', op. cit., p. 198.

[48] *Emile*, Livre IV, in *Oeuvres Complètes*, Vol. IV, Bibliothèque de la Pléiade (Paris, 1969), pp. 497-8.

[49] *'Préface'* to *Le Cabinet des Antiques et Gambara*, in *Contes Drolatiques*, Bibliothèque de la Pléiade (Paris, 1965), p. 368.

[50] The relevant passages from the official documents are reproduced in Henri d'Alméras, *Paul et Virginie de Bernardin de Saint-Pierre* (Paris: Malfère, 1937), pp. 62-71.

[51] Ibid., p. 68.

[52] Ibid., pp. 70-1.

[53] Ibid., p. 62; *Paul et Virginie*, ed. P. Trahard, op. cit., p. 206.

[54] Summarized in C. Benoit, 'Les Origines Historiques du Roman de Paul et Virginie de Bernardin de Saint-Pierre', *Annales de l'Est*, V (1891), pp. 485-96.

[55] *Paul et Virginie*, ed. P. Trahard, op. cit., p. clvii.

[56] *Voyage à l'Ile de France*, op. cit., Vol. I, p. 159.

[57] Ibid., pp. 201-7.

[58] Ibid., p. 228.

[59] Ibid., p. 148.

[60] M. Souriau, *Bernardin de Saint-Pierre*, op. cit., p. 231.

[61] Marie-Thérèse Veyrenc, *Edition Critique du Manuscrit de Paul et Virginie* (Paris: Nizet, 1975); Gustave Lanson, 'Un Manuscrit de Paul et Virginie', in *Etudes d' Histoire Littéraire* (Paris: Champion, 1930); *Paul et Virginie*, ed. P. Trahard, op. cit., pp. lxv-cxxxiv.

[62] M. Souriau, *Bernardin de Saint-Pierre*, op. cit., p. 231.

[63] *Etudes de la Nature*, in *Oeuvres Complètes*, op. cit., Vol. V, p. 87.

Paul and Virginia

The Ile de France

Preface to the 1788 Edition

I wrote this little book with great aims in view. In it I have tried to paint a soil and a vegetation different from those of Europe. Our poets have for long enough made their lovers rest on the banks of streams, in meadows and beneath the leaves of beeches. Mine were to sit on the seashore, at the foot of high rocks, in the shade of coconut-palms, banana-trees and lemon-trees in flower. The other part of the world wants only Theocrituses and Virgils to provide us with pictures at least as worthy of interest as those of our own country. I know that certain travellers who are also men of taste have given us enchanting descriptions of several islands of the southern ocean; but the manners of their inhabitants, and still more those of the Europeans who land there, are often a blot on the landscape. I wished to join to the beauty of nature between the tropics the moral beauty of a little society. It was also my purpose to exhibit a number of great truths, among them this one : that our happiness consists in living according to Nature and virtue. But, in order to portray happy families, I did not find it necessary to invent a novel. I can assure the reader that those I speak of did really exist, and that their story is true so far as its principal events are concerned. Several settlers whom I knew on the Ile de France testified to their authenticity. I have added no more than a few details insignificant in themselves but drawn from my personal experience and possessing reality by that very fact. When, some years ago, I had made a very imperfect sketch of this species of pastoral, I asked if I might read it to a beautiful lady who was much received in wealthy and distinguished society and to some grave men who lived far from it, so that I might form an idea of the effect it would produce on readers of such different kinds : I had the satisfaction of seeing them all shed tears. This was the only judgement I was able to extract from them, and it was all that I wished to know. But as a great vice often walks close on the heels of a small talent, this success inspired me with the vanity to give to my work the title of *Nature's Portrait*. Happily, I remembered how little I know of Nature even in the climate where I was born, how rich, varied, lovely, magnificent and mysterious she is in those countries where I have looked on her works only as a traveller, and how unfurnished I am with the acuteness, taste and powers of expression that are necessary to know and to paint her. And so, after further reflection, I included this feeble attempt under the name and at the end of my *Studies of Nature* which the public has received with such kindness, so that this title, by recalling my incapacity, might serve as a perpetual reminder of its indulgence.

Jacques-Henri Bernardin de Saint-Pierre

Paul and Virginia

On the eastern slope of the mountain that rises behind the town of Port Louis on the Ile de France may be seen, on a piece of ground once under cultivation, the remains of two small cabins. They stand almost in the centre of a broad valley bordered by high rocks with a single opening towards the north. To the left, with the town of Port Louis at its base, appears the mountain called Discovery Hill, from which the signal is given when a vessel puts in at the island; to the right a road leads from the town to the Pamplemousses district; farther on, the church of the same name, with its avenues of bamboo, can be seen rising from the middle of a wide plain, and farther still the edge of a forest that stretches to the very ends of the island. Straight ahead, the shore curves along the edge of Tomb Bay; a little to the right is the Cape of Misfortune and beyond it the open sea, on the surface of which a few uninhabited islets can be made out, among them the Coin de Mire, which seems like a bastion amidst the waves.

At the entrance to the valley, from which so many things can be seen, the echoes from the mountain repeat unceasingly the sound of the wind that stirs the nearby forests and the crash of the waves as they break on the far-off reefs; but beside the cabins themselves no sound can be heard and round about one sees only the high rocks rising sheer like the walls of a fortress. Clumps of trees grow at the foot of these rocks, in their crevices and even on their summits where clouds gather. The rains that are attracted to their peaks often paint their green and brown sides with the colours of the rainbow, and at their base feed the springs which form the source of the little Latania River. Within their precincts a profound silence reigns: all is tranquil, the air, the waters and the light. The echo barely repeats the whispering of the palmettos that grow on the high rock shelves, their long spears swaying constantly in the wind. On the floor of the valley the light is soft, for the sun's rays reach it only at midday; but from the first moment of dawn they strike the encircling peaks, which rise above the shadows of the mountain, and make them appear gold and purple against the azure of the sky.

I loved to visit this place where I could enjoy at once a boundless view and the deepest solitude. One day, whilst I was seated beside the cabins and contemplating their ruined condition, a man well advanced in years passed by. He was dressed, according to the fashion of the older settlers of the island, in a short jacket and long pants. He was barefoot and leaned upon a staff of ebony as he walked. His hair was pure white, his countenance frank and noble. I greeted him respectfully. He returned my greeting and, having considered me a moment, came near and sat down to rest on the little hillock where I was seated. Encouraged by this show of confidence, I spoke to him: 'Father,' said I, 'can you tell me to whom these two cabins belonged?'

'My son,' he replied, 'twenty years ago these tumbledown dwellings and this unploughed land were a place of happiness for the two families that lived here. Theirs is a touching story. But can the fate of a few obscure individuals on an island on the route to the Indies be of interest to a European? Who would wish to live here poor and unknown, even if happiness were his reward? Men want to know only the history of the great and of kings, which is of no use to anyone.'

'Father,' I continued, 'it is evident from your bearing and your conversation that you are a man of great experience. Pray tell me, if you have the leisure, what you know of those who once lived in this wild place and be assured that even the man who is most depraved by wordly prejudices likes to hear of the happiness provided by Nature and virtue.'

And so, after pressing his hands to his forehead as if seeking to recall many sundry details, the old man told me this story.

In the year 1726 a young man from Normandy, Monsieur de la

Tour, after fruitless attempts to obtain a commission in France and vain requests for the assistance of his family, determined to come to this island to seek his fortune. He had with him a young wife whom he loved dearly and who loved him in return. She belonged to a rich and ancient family of his province, but had married him in secret and without dowry; he was not of noble birth and her relations had opposed their union. Leaving her in the town of Port Louis on this island, he took ship for Madagascar, intending to buy some slaves and to return here without delay to establish a plantation. He reached Madagascar around the middle of October, at the beginning of the bad season, and not long afterwards he died, a victim of the pestilential fevers that rage there during six months of the year and which will always prevent European nations from settling permanently. The effects he had brought with him were dispersed after his death, the common fate of those who die outside their native country. His wife, who had stayed behind, found herself widowed and with child on an island where she had neither credit nor recommendation; her sole wordly possession was a Negress. Declining to seek the aid of any man after the death of him she had loved to the exclusion of all others, she drew courage from her misfortune and resolved to cultivate with her slave a small piece of ground to provide the necessities of life.

The island was almost uninhabited then and land to be had for the taking; yet she chose neither the most fertile districts nor those best adapted to commerce; instead, seeking some mountain gorge, some hidden retreat where she could live alone and unnoticed, she turned her steps from the town towards these rocks, where she might shelter as in a nest. All sensitive and suffering creatures, from a common instinct, seek refuge in the wildest and most deserted places, as if high rocks could form ramparts against adversity and the serenity of nature bring peace to a troubled and unhappy soul. But Providence, which comes to our aid when we desire no more than is necessary for our well-being, had in store for Madame de la Tour an advantage which neither wealth nor rank can give – a friend.

For a year past there had been living in this place a good woman named Marguerite who was both lively and tender-hearted. She had been born in Brittany into a simple peasant family who loved her dearly and with whom she would have been happy had she not foolishly put her trust in the love of a nobleman of the neighbourhood. He had promised her marriage but, having satisfied his passion, had abandoned her, refusing even to provide for his child which she was soon to bear. Thereupon she determined to leave for ever the village where she had been born and to go and hide her misdeed in the colonies far from the country where she had lost the only dowry of a poor and honest girl, her good name. She borrowed a small sum, enough to acquire an old Negro, and together they cultivated a little corner of this district.

Her Negress close behind her, Madame de la Tour reached this spot to find Marguerite with her baby at her breast. She was pleased to meet a woman in a position which she judged to be similar to her own, and in few words she described her past condition and present needs. Marguerite was moved to pity by her narrative, and desiring to win the confidence rather than the esteem of her new acquaintance, she confessed to her, concealing nothing, the indiscretion of which she herself was guilty. 'My fate was deserved,' she said, 'but you, Madame, have been honest and unfortunate.' And, shedding tears, she offered her both shelter and friendship. Touched by so affectionate a welcome, Madame de la Tour embraced her, saying : 'Ah ! God must want to put an end to my affliction, for He inspires you, to whom I am a stranger, with more goodness to me than ever I found in my own family.'

I was acquainted with Marguerite, and although I live a league and a half from here in the wood on the other side of the Long Mountain, I considered myself her neighbour. In the cities of Europe, a street, a mere wall, is sufficient to keep apart members of the same family for years on end; but in the new colonies we consider as neighbours those who are separated from us by no more than woods and mountains. At that time especially, before the increase in trade to the Indies, simply living nearby was grounds for friendship, and hospitality to strangers a duty and a pleasure; so that when I learned that my neighbour had a companion, I called to see if I could be of service to them. In Madame de la Tour I found a woman whose noble and melancholy countenance stirred my interest. She was then very near her delivery. I advised the two ladies that, in the interests of their children, but above all to prevent anyone else from settling there, they should divide between them the floor of this valley, which covers about twenty acres. They put the task of dividing it in my hands. I marked out two more or less equal portions, one comprising the upper part of this enclosure from the peak of that cloud-covered rock where the Latania River has its source to the opening you can see high up where the mountain slopes sharply and which, from its resemblance to a cannon-opening in a parapet, is called the Embrasure. The ground in this part is so rocky and veined with ravines that one can hardly walk on it, but it produces tall trees and is filled with springs and little streams. I included in the other portion all the lower half of the valley lying along the Latania River as far as this opening where we are sitting, from which the river begins its descent between those two hills to the sea. You can still see a few strips of meadow-land on this lower part; the ground is mostly level but it has little advantage over the other, for in the rainy season it becomes marshy and in the dry spells as hard as lead: to dig a trench you have first to break up the earth with an axe.

The land thus divided into two parts, I invited the ladies to draw lots for them. The upper part fell to Madame de la Tour, the lower to Marguerite. Each was content with her portion, though they particularly requested me not to separate their dwellings. 'In that way,' they said, 'we shall always be able to see and talk to each other and give each other help.' Yet each one needed a place she could retire to privately. Marguerite's little cabin stood in the centre of the valley, on the very limits of her land; just beside it, on Madame de la Tour's, I built another: there the two friends were near neighbours yet each was on her own property. I cut the logs myself on the mountain-side and carried latania leaves from the seashore to construct these two cabins, which now, as you see, have neither door nor roof – yet still, alas! only too much remains for my memory to work upon. Time, which so quickly destroys the monuments of empires, seems in this wilderness to spare those of friendship and thus to perpetuate my sorrows to the end of my days.

The second cabin was hardly finished when Madame de la
Tour was delivered of a girl. I had served as godfather for Marguerite's child, who was named Paul; and now Madame de la
Tour desired that her friend and myself should jointly choose a
name for her daughter. Marguerite gave her the name Virginia.
'She will be virtuous,' she said, 'and she will be happy. I met misfortune only when I wandered from the path of virtue.'

When Madame de la Tour was recovered from her confinement
the two little settlements began to show some return, thanks to the
attention I was able to give from time to time but above all to the
unremitting labour of the slaves. Domingue, Marguerite's Yolof
Negro, although no longer young, was still strong and active and
joined experience to his native good sense. He cultivated the
ground that seemed to him most fertile, whether on Marguerite's
property or Madame de la Tour's, choosing for each place the most
suitable kind of seed. He sowed millet and maize where the soil
was inferior, a bit of wheat on the best ground, rice in the low-
lying marshes, and, at the foot of the rocks, pumpkins, marrows
and cucumbers, which like something to climb on. He planted
sweet-potatoes on dry ground where they grow sweetest of all,
cotton on the high places, sugar-cane where the soil is heavy and
coffee plants on the hillsides where they produce a bean that is
small but of excellent quality. Along the river and around the
cabins he set banana-trees, which give long clusters of fruit and
cooling shade all the year round, and a few tobacco plants to
lighten his hours of care and those of his good mistresses. He went
to cut firewood on the mountain and here and there broke up
rocks to level the paths. He performed all these tasks with intelligence and energy because he was eager to serve. He was strongly
attached to Marguerite and hardly less so to Madame de la Tour,
whose Negress he had married when Virginia was born. She was
called Marie and he loved her passionately. She had been born
in Madagascar and had brought with her some of the crafts of her
birthplace, especially the weaving of baskets and of the stuffs called
pagnes from the grasses that grow in the woods. Skilful, neat and
very faithful, she saw to the preparation of meals, raised a few

chickens and from time to time went to Port Louis to sell what the two families produced in excess of their needs, which was indeed very little. If to these you add a pair of goats that were reared alongside the children and a big dog that watched outside at night you will have an idea of the entire household and revenue of these two little farms.

The two friends spun cotton from morning to evening, maintaining themselves and their families by this work. Otherwise, so unfurnished were they with the goods of civilization that they went barefoot about the settlements, putting on shoes only on Sunday to go to early-morning mass in the church at Pamplemousses, which you can see over there in the distance. This church is much further away than Port Louis, but they seldom went to the town, afraid of being scorned because they dressed in the coarse blue Bengal cloth usually worn by slaves. But what is public consideration compared to domestic happiness? If these two ladies had to endure some slights abroad, their pleasure was the greater on returning home. No sooner would Marie and Domingue, standing on this high point, catch sight of them on the road from Pamplemousses, than they would hasten to the foot of the mountain to help them up the sloping path, their joy at seeing their mistresses again showing clearly in their eyes. At home they found cleanliness and freedom, possessions that they owed to no labour but their own, and eager and affectionate servants. Between themselves there was a bond of common need; the injuries they had suffered were of nearly the same kind. With one another they used the tender names of friend, companion and sister; they had but one will, one interest, one table. Everything was shared between them. And if fires older and keener than those of friendship sometimes reawakened in their hearts, a pure religion and their habitual chastity guided them towards another life, just as the flame, having consumed its earthly fuel, takes flight for heaven.

The duties laid upon them by Nature were a source of additional happiness. Their mutual affection redoubled at the sight of their children, each of whom was the fruit of an unfortunate love. They delighted to bathe them together and to put them to sleep in the same cradle; often one would give her milk to the other's child.

'Dear friend,' Madame de la Tour would say, 'each of us will have
two children and each of our children will have two mothers.' As
two buds left on two trees of the same kind, when all their
branches have been broken by the storm, will bring forth sweeter
fruit if each is taken from the maternal trunk and grafted upon its
neighbour, so these two infants, deprived of all other relations,
were filled with sentiments more tender than those of son and
daughter, brother and sister, when they were exchanged at the
breast by the two friends who had given them life. Already, over
their cradles, their mothers were talking of the day when they
would marry; and, assuaging their own grief with this prospect of
conjugal felicity, they were very often brought to tears, one remembering that her injuries were the result of having neglected the
laws of marriage, the other of having submitted to them; one had
suffered for having reached above her condition, the other for
having married beneath hers. But they comforted themselves with
the thought that their children, luckier than they, would one day
enjoy the pleasures of love and the happiness of equality far from
the cruel prejudices of Europe.

Indeed nothing could compare to the attachment they already
displayed. If Paul happened to fret, Virginia would be brought
and at her sight he would smile and be pacified. If Virginia were
in pain, it was Paul's cries that made it known, but the dear child
would instantly conceal her suffering so as not to cause him distress.
I never came here without finding them both naked, as is the
custom in this country, scarcely able to walk and supporting each
other by the hands and under the arms, like a picture of the twins
in the constellation Gemini. Even the night could not part them;
they would often be found lying in the same cradle, cheeks and
breasts pressed together, their hands round each other's neck,
embracing as they slept.

When they were able to speak, the first words they learned to
exchange were 'brother' and 'sister'; and childhood, if it knows
tenderer caresses, knows no sweeter names. Their upbringing only
strengthened their attachment by fostering a sense of reciprocal
need. All that belonged to the management and good order of the
household and the preparation of their simple fare soon became

Virginia's province, and her efforts were always rewarded with
compliments and kisses from her brother. On his side there was
restless activity: he would dig the garden with Domingue or, a
little axe in hand, follow him into the woods; and if on these out-
ings he spied a pretty flower, a tempting fruit or a bird's nest,
even at the very top of a tree, he would climb up and bring them
to his sister.

Wherever one of them was to be found, the other was sure to
be close by. One day, as I was coming down from the top of this
mountain, I noticed Virginia running from the end of the garden
towards the house, the back of her petticoat thrown up over her
head as protection against a sudden shower. From a distance I
thought she was alone, but as I came forward to give her my arm I
saw that she was holding Paul's – he was entirely covered by the
same canopy – and that they were laughing, both of them, to be
sheltering together under an umbrella of their own invention. The
sight of these two pretty heads encircled by the billowing petticoat
brought to my mind the children of Leda, enclosed in the same
shell.

They had no other studies but helping and pleasing each other;
they were as ignorant as Creoles and could neither read nor write.
What had taken place long ago and in far-away countries troubled
them not at all; their curiosity did not reach beyond this mountain.
They believed that the world ended at the limits of their island
and they imagined no pleasant places or things beyond its shores.
Their affection for each other and for their mothers entirely
occupied their hearts. Never had useless learning made them shed
tears; never had the teachings of a gloomy morality filled them
with anxiety. They did not know that they must not steal, as the
two households held everything in common; nor be intemperate,
having as much wholesome food as they wanted; nor tell lies,
having nothing to conceal. They had never been frightened by
stories of the terrible punishments prepared by God for ungrateful
children; their mothers' affection had bred like feelings in them.
What they had been taught of religion made them love it; and if
they did not make lengthy prayers in church, no matter where
they were – at home, in the fields or in the woods – they lifted up

to heaven innocent hands and hearts full of love for their parents.

Thus did their early years pass like a lovely dawn which gives promise of a lovelier day. Already they shared with their mothers all the duties of the household. As soon as the crowing cock announced the return of the day, Virginia would rise and go to fetch water at the nearby spring, before returning to the house to prepare breakfast. Soon after, when the surrounding peaks were tipped with gold by the rising sun, Marguerite and her son would come to Madame de la Tour's cabin and together they would all offer a prayer before the first meal of the day. Often they would eat it outdoors, sitting on the grass under a bower of banana-trees whose substantial fruit furnished them with a dish ready-prepared and whose long, broad and glossy leaves served as linen for their table. Nourishing food in abundance caused the children's bodies to grow rapidly and, as could be seen in their faces, a mild upbringing had brought purity and contentment to their souls. Virginia was only twelve years old, but already her figure was more than half formed. Long blonde hair framed her head; her blue eyes and coral lips glowed softly against the freshness of her skin; when she spoke they always smiled in concert, but when she was silent the natural inclination of her eyes towards heaven gave her face an expression of extreme, even somewhat melancholy, sensitivity. With Paul, a manly nature seemed to be developing amidst the graces of adolescence. He was taller than Virginia, his complexion darker, his nose more aquiline; his eyes, which were black, might have revealed a touch of pride had not long lashes, spreading round them like the fine hairs of a paintbrush, given them an air of exceeding gentleness. In spite of his perpetual activity, a tranquillity would come over him at the appearance of his sister and he would go and sit beside her. Often an entire meal would pass without the exchange of a word between them. Their silence, the simple grace of their posture and the beauty of their bare feet would have made you think of a classical sculpture in white marble representing two of Niobe's children; and yet their eyes, constantly seeking each other, their smiles, answered by more tender smiles, made them seem like those children of heaven, those blessed spirits whose very nature is mutual love and who need no thoughts to render their feelings nor words for their affection.

As she watched her daughter develop with so many charms Madame de la Tour felt her anxiety increase with her fondness. She would say to me sometimes: 'What would become of Virginia if I were to die and leave her without fortune?'

She had in France an aged maiden aunt, rich, pious and of noble family, who had so cruelly refused to help her when she had married Monsieur de la Tour that she had resolved never again to apply to her, no matter how extreme her need. But now that she was a mother, she no longer feared the humiliation of a refusal. She wrote to her aunt telling her of her husband's unexpected death, the birth of her daughter and the difficulties of her position, far from her own country, deprived of all assistance and with a child to care for. She received no reply. Being of a noble nature, she was not afraid to abase herself or expose herself to the reproaches of a relation who had never forgiven her for marrying a humbly-born (though virtuous) man. She continued therefore to write at every opportunity in the hope of arousing her aunt's compassion for Virginia; but many years had passed without the slightest sign of her concern.

At last, in 1738, Madame de la Tour learned that Monsieur de la Bourdonnais, who had been appointed governor of the island three years previously, had a letter from her aunt to give her. Little caring, this time, that she was poorly dressed, she hurried to Port Louis, her happiness for her child making her indifferent to the censure of the inhabitants. Monsieur de la Bourdonnais had indeed a letter for her from her aunt. The old woman informed her niece that she deserved her fate for marrying an adventurer and a libertine, that the passions carried with them their own punishment, that her husband's early death was a just correction from Heaven, that she had done well to take herself to an island colony rather than disgrace her family in France, and that, as for fortune, she was in a country where all but the idle could become rich. Having condemned her thus, she ended by praising herself. The consequences of marriage were often grievous, she said, and to avoid these she had always refused to marry. The truth is that, being ambitious, she had wanted none but a husband of high rank; yet despite her riches and the indifference of those at court to everything but fortune, no one could be found to accept an alliance with so ugly and hard-hearted a young woman.

She added in a postscript that, on reflection, she had strongly recommended her niece to Monsieur de la Bourdonnais. This she had indeed done, but in a manner only too common nowadays, which makes a protector more to be feared than even a declared enemy: to justify her harshness in the governor's eyes, she had blackened her niece's character whilst feigning pity for her distress.

No disinterested man could view Madame de la Tour without respect and concern, but Monsieur de la Bourdonnais had been prejudiced against her and she was very coldly received. To the account she gave of her own and her daughter's circumstances his replies were short and curt: ' I shall see ... we shall see ... perhaps in time ... there are many unfortunate people ... your aunt is a very respectable woman, why trouble her? ... it is you who are at fault.'

Madame de la Tour returned to the settlement, her heart heavy with grief and full of bitterness. When she arrived she sat down, threw her aunt's letter on the table and said to her friend: 'There is my reward for eleven years' patience!' But as she alone could read in their little society, she took up the letter and read it aloud before the assembled family. She had hardly finished when Marguerite broke out: 'What need have we of your relations? God is our only true father, and has He abandoned us? Have we not lived happily until now? Why do you vex yourself? Have you no courage?' And seeing that Madame de la Tour was weeping, she fell on her neck and, pressing her closely in her arms, cried: 'My dear, dear friend,' her own voice choking with sobs. Virginia, melting to tears at this spectacle, pressed now her mother's, now Marguerite's hands to her lips and her heart; and Paul, his eyes glowing with anger, cried out, clenched his fists and stamped his foot, not knowing whom to blame. The noise at once brought Marie and Domingue, and soon the cabin was filled with wailing:

'Oh, Madame! . . . my good mistress! . . . my dear mother! . . . do not weep!' At these tender proofs of affection Madame de la Tour's grief vanished; taking Paul and Virginia in her arms, she said contentedly: 'My children, you may be the cause of my sorrow, but you are the source of all my joy. Oh my dear children, it was from far away that my trouble came; here around me all is happiness.' Paul and Virginia did not understand her words, but they smiled when they saw that her tranquillity had returned and fell to embracing her. And so their happiness was restored as if after a storm in a season of fine weather.

Each day saw an increase in the natural goodness of the children's dispositions. One Sunday at dawn, while their mothers were at early mass in the church at Pamplemousses, an escaped Negress appeared beneath the banana-trees surrounding the cabins. She was as emaciated as a skeleton and wore nothing but a shred of coarse cloth wrapped round her loins. Throwing herself down before Virginia, who was preparing breakfast for the family, she said: 'Young lady, have pity on a poor runaway slave; I have been wandering in these mountains for a month, half dead with hunger and many times pursued by hunters and their dogs. I escaped from my master, a rich planter in the Black River district; see for yourself how he treated me;' and she showed Virginia her body which was furrowed with deep scars from the whippings she had received. 'I was going to drown myself,' she added, 'but knowing that you lived here, I said to myself: "I needn't die yet; there are still some good white people in this country." '

Virginia was much affected: 'Have no fear, you unfortunate creature,' she replied. 'Here, eat this,' and she gave her the breakfast she had made ready for the family. In a few minutes the slave had devoured it completely. Seeing that she was satisfied, Virginia said: 'Poor wretch; I must go to your master and ask him to pardon you; when he sees your condition he will be moved to pity. Will you lead me to him?'

'Angel of God,' answered the Negress, 'I will follow you where-ever you like.'

Virginia called her brother and asked him to accompany them. The slave led them along paths and through woods, across high mountains which they climbed with much difficulty and broad rivers which they were obliged to ford. At length, towards midday, they reached the foot of a hill on the banks of the Black River. Before them were extensive fields, a solidly-built house and numerous slaves engaged in various sorts of labour. Their master went about among them, a pipe in his mouth and a cane in his hand. He was a tall and forbidding man with olive skin and black brows that met above a pair of sunken eyes. Holding Paul by the arm and quaking inwardly, Virginia approached the landowner and begged him, for the love of God, to pardon his slave, who remained a few paces behind them. At first the man paid little attention to these two shabbily dressed children, but when he noticed Virginia's graceful figure and her beautiful blonde hair under the hood of her blue cloak, when he heard the softness of her voice, which trembled (as indeed her whole body did) as she asked for pardon, he took his pipe from his mouth and, lifting up his cane to heaven, he swore a dreadful oath that he would grant his pardon not for the love of God but for love of her. Virginia quickly signalled to the slave to approach her master; then she fled, and Paul hurried after her.

Together they made their way up the slope of the hill down which they had come and, having reached the top, sat down under a tree overcome with weariness, hunger and thirst. Since sunrise they had travelled more than five leagues on an empty stomach. Paul said to Virginia : 'Sister, it is past noon; you are hungry and thirsty and we shall find nothing here for our dinner; let us go down again and ask the slave's master for something to eat.'

'Oh no, my dear,' replied Virginia, 'I am too frightened of him. Remember what Mamma sometimes says : "The bread of the wicked fills the mouth with gravel." '

'What shall we do, then?' said Paul. 'The fruit of these trees is not good to eat; there is not so much as a lemon or a tamarind here to refresh you.'

'God will have pity on us,' replied Virginia. 'He answers the cries of the little birds when they ask Him for food.' No sooner had she spoken these words than they heard the sound of a spring tumbling from a nearby rock. They ran to it and quenched their thirst with water that was clearer than crystal, then gathered and ate a bit of the cress that grew on its banks.

As they looked about them, trying to find some more substantial nourishment, Virginia spied a young cabbage-palm amongst the other trees of the forest. The kernel that is enclosed in the leaves at the top of this tree is an excellent food; but although the trunk was no thicker than a man's leg, it was more than sixty feet high. The wood of this type of palm is in fact no more than a mass of small fibres, but its sapwood is so hard that it turns the edge of the sharpest axe, and Paul had not even a knife. He thought of setting fire to the base of the tree but here too there was an obstacle : he had no steel, and what is more, although the island is covered with rocks, I doubt whether there is a single piece of flint to be found on it. But necessity breeds ingenuity, and the most useful inventions have often been the work of the neediest men. Paul determined to light a fire using the native method : with the sharp end of a stone he made a small hole in a thoroughly dry branch, which he placed under his feet; using the edge of the stone, he sharpened to a point another dry branch of a different sort of wood; then he put the pointed piece of wood into the little hole in the branch under his feet and, rolling it rapidly back and forth between his hands as one does with a mill for whipping chocolate, he soon saw smoke and sparks coming from the point of contact. He gathered dry grass and more branches and set fire to the foot of the palm-tree, which soon fell with a great crash. The fire also served to remove the long, woody covering of prickly leaves from the cabbage. They ate part of it raw, and part cooked under the embers, and found them equally savoury. As they made their frugal meal they were filled with joy at the thought of the good action they had performed that morning, but their happiness was troubled by the anxiety they knew their long absence would be causing their mothers. Virginia returned often to this theme but Paul, feeling that he had recovered his strength, assured her that it would not be long before they set their parents' minds at ease.

After dinner they found themselves at a loss how to begin, for

they had no one to guide them on their way home. But Paul was
not easily disconcerted. He said to Virginia : 'Our cabin lies towards the sun at midday; do you see that mountain with the three
peaks in the distance? We must go over it as we did this morning.
Come, my dear, let us set off.' This mountain was the one called
the Three Paps, from the shape of its three peaks. They descended
the northern slope of Black River Hill and, after walking for an
hour, found themselves on the banks of a broad river which barred
their way. That part of the island is entirely covered with great
forests and is so little known even today that several of its mountains and rivers have not yet been named. The river on whose banks
they were standing rushes in a foaming torrent over a bed of rocks.
The noise of the water so frightened Virginia that she was afraid
to wade across. So Paul took her on his back. Stepping from one
slippery stone to another, he carried her over the turbulent water
to the other side, telling her as he went : 'Don't be afraid; with you
I feel very strong. If the owner of the plantation had refused to
pardon his slave for you, I would have fought with him.'

'Fought with that big and wicked man?' cried Virginia. 'What
danger I led you into! Oh Heaven! how hard it is to do a good
deed! It is only evil that is easy.'

When Paul reached the opposite bank he wanted to continue
the journey with his sister on his back, imagining that he could
carry her to the top of the Three Paps, which he could see at a
distance of half a league ahead of them, but his strength soon
failed and he was obliged to put her down and to sit beside her on
the ground to rest. Virginia said to him : 'Brother, the sun is low
in the sky; you still have some strength left but mine is altogether
gone; let me stay here while you return home to reassure our
mothers.' 'Oh no,' said Paul, 'I shan't leave you. If night comes
upon us in these woods, I shall light a fire and fell a cabbage-
palm; you can eat the kernel and with the leaves I can make an
ajoupa to shelter you.' But when Virginia had rested a little, she
gathered some long leaves of hart's-tongue which hung from the
trunk of an old tree that leaned over the river and fashioned a kind
of boot by wrapping them round her feet, which were bleeding
from the stones of the paths; for in her eagerness to be of service she

had forgotten to put on shoes. Soothed by the coolness of the leaves, she broke a stick of bamboo and set off, supporting herself with one hand on the bamboo cane and with the other on Paul.

In this manner they made their way slowly through the woods; but the height of the trees and the thickness of the foliage soon made them lose sight of the Three Paps, which had given them their direction, and even of the sun, which was already beginning to set. After some time they strayed, without noticing it, from the beaten track they had been following and found themselves in a labyrinth of trees, creepers and rocks which had no outlet. Paul made Virginia sit down and began to run here and there, quite beside himself, looking for some way out of the dense thicket; but he only tired himself in vain. He climbed to the top of a tall tree, from which he hoped at least to locate the Three Paps, but in every direction he could see nothing but tree-tops, some of them alight with the last rays of the setting sun. The shadow of the mountain was already covering the wooded valleys, and the wind was dropping, as it does at sunset; a profound and lonely silence reigned, broken only by the belling of the stags that came to seek a lair in these remote places. Hoping that some hunter would hear his voice, Paul cried out with all his strength : 'Come, come and help Virginia !' But only the echoes of the forest answered him, repeating again and again : 'Virginia ! . . . Virginia !'

Overcome by fatigue and vexation, Paul got down from the tree and looked about for some means of passing the night where they were, but there was neither spring nor cabbage-palm nor even a dry branch he could use to light a fire. His experience told him just how meagre were the resources at his disposal and he began to weep.

'Don't cry, my dear,' said Virginia, 'or I shall be overwhelmed with sorrow. I am the cause of all your distress and of what our mothers must be feeling now as well. We should do nothing, not even good, without consulting our parents. How thoughtless I've been.' At these words she burst into tears, saying to Paul : 'Let us pray, brother, and God will have pity on us.' They had hardly finished their prayers when they heard the barking of a dog. 'It must belong to some hunter who comes here at dusk to lie in wait for deer,' said Paul. Soon the barking grew louder and more frequent. 'It sounds like Fidele, our house-dog,' said Virginia, 'yes, I recognize his voice. Can we have returned as far as the foot of our own mountain?' A moment later Fidele – for it was he – was at their feet, barking, howling, groaning and overwhelming them with caresses. Before they could recover from their surprise, they caught sight of Domingue running towards them. As he reached them the children saw that the good Negro was weeping for joy and this started their own tears, so that they were unable to utter a word.

'Oh my young masters,' said Domingue when he had recovered himself, 'how worried your mothers have been! How astonished they were not to find you when they returned from mass! I had accompanied them to church and Marie, who was working at a spot far from the cabins, could not say where you had gone. I rushed from one place to another all over the settlements, having no idea myself where to look for you. Finally I got some of your old clothes and let Fidele take your scent from them. The poor beast seemed to understand me for he immediately set off on your trail. He led me, his tail wagging all the while, to the Black River. There I learned from a planter that you had returned a runaway slave to him and that he had pardoned her at your request. But what a cruel pardon it was! for he showed her to me chained by the foot to a block of wood, an iron collar with three hooks fastened round her neck. From there Fidele followed your scent to a spring on Black River Hill, where he stopped, barking with all his might; a cabbage-palm had been felled nearby and a fire was still smoking. At last he led me here. We are at the foot of the Three Paps and still a good four leagues from home. Come, you must eat something to regain your strength.' He then set before them a cake, some fruit and a large gourd filled with a mixture of water, wine, lemon juice, sugar and nutmeg, a beverage which their mothers had prepared to refresh and fortify them. Virginia sighed as she thought of the poor slave and of their mothers' anxiety, repeating several times, 'Oh, how hard it is to do good!'

While she and Paul were refreshing themselves, Domingue lit a fire. Among the rocks he found a twisted shrub called round-wood, which burns with a bright flame even while still green. With this he made a torch and set it alight, for night had already fallen. But when it was time to set off he was faced with a much greater difficulty: the children's feet had become so red and swollen that they were unable to walk. Domingue could not decide whether to go the long distance necessary to fetch help or to spend the night with them in the forest. 'There was a time,' he said, 'when I carried you both in my arms at once, but I am old now and you are no longer small.' While he stood thus perplexed, a band of runaway slaves came into view not twenty paces from where they were. The leader of the band approached and said to Paul and Virginia: 'Don't be afraid, good white children. We saw you pass this morning with a Negress from the Black River; you were going to ask her wicked master to pardon her. To show our gratitude we will carry you home on our shoulders.' At a sign from him four of the sturdiest runaways bound some branches together with creepers to make a stretcher, placed Paul and Virginia on it and lifted them to their shoulders; then, Domingue walking ahead with the torch, they set off, all the band shouting with joy and heaping good wishes on the children. Virginia was touched. 'Oh, my dear friend!' she said to Paul, 'God never lets a good action go unrewarded.'

It was nearly midnight when they arrived at the foot of their mountain to see that fires had been lit on several of the rounded crests. They had hardly begun their ascent when they heard voices crying: 'Is that you, children?' 'Yes,' they and the slaves shouted together, 'it is us.' Soon they saw their mothers and Marie coming to meet them with flaming torches. 'Where have you been, you thoughtless children?' said Madame de la Tour. 'Do you know the anguish you have caused us?'

'We've been to the Black River,' said Virginia, 'to ask pardon for a poor runaway slave. It was to her that I gave our breakfast this morning because she was starving, and now these runaways have brought us home.' Unable to speak, Madame de la Tour embraced her daughter. When she felt her cheeks wet with her mother's tears, Virginia said: 'I am repaid for all that I endured.'

Marguerite, beside herself with joy, clasped Paul in her arms,

saying: 'My son, you too have performed a good action.' When
they were once again under their own roofs with their children,
they gave an abundant supper to the runaway slaves, who afterwards returned to the forests wishing them every good fortune.

Each day was a day of peace and happiness for the two families.
Neither envy nor ambition tormented them. They had no desire
to have in the world outside the kind of empty reputation that is
got by intrigue and lost by slander; they were content to be their
own witnesses and their own judges. On this island where, as in
all European colonies, malicious gossip is the only topic of interest,
their virtues and even their names were unknown; yet when a
passer-by on the road to Pamplemousses would ask the settlers of
the plain: 'Who lives in those little cabins on the mountain?' they
would reply without ever having met them: 'They are good
people.' So, from under thorny bushes, do violets send out their
sweet perfume, though they remain unseen.

They had banished from their conversation that evil-speaking
which, under the appearance of justice, always inclines the heart
either to hatred or to duplicity; for it is impossible not to hate men
if we believe them to be wicked, or to live with wicked men without
falsely concealing our hatred behind the outward forms of goodwill. Speaking ill of others thus forces us to be on bad terms either
with them or with ourselves. Without passing judgement on individuals, their talk was all of ways of doing good to people in general,
and although they had not the means, they had a constant will to
do so, which filled them with a benevolence ever ready to reach
beyond their circle. Solitude, far from having made them barbarous, had made them more humane. If the scandals of society
provided no matter for their conversation, the study of nature
filled them with wonder and delight. They were transported with
admiration for the power of a Providence which, by their hands,
had spread plenty and graces amidst these barren rocks and provided them with pleasures that were simple, pure and ever-
renewed.

At twelve years of age Paul was more robust and intelligent than

Europeans at fifteen, and where the Negro Domingue had merely cultivated, he had beautified. He went with him to the neighbouring woods to uproot young lemon- and orange-trees, tamarinds whose round tops are of such a lovely green, and custard-apple trees whose fruit contains a sweet cream with the fragrance of orange-blossoms. He set these trees, which had already grown quite tall, around the perimeter of their enclosure, where he had already planted the seeds of those trees that flower or fruit in their second year : the agathis whose long bunches of white flowers hang down in a circle like the crystals of a chandelier; the Persian lilac whose clusters of blossoms, the colour of unbleached linen, rise straight into the air; and the papaw whose trunk bristles with green melons instead of branches and rises to a capital of broad leaves like those of the fig-tree.

Besides these, he had planted the pips and kernels of myrobalans, mangoes, avocados, guavas, jack-fruits and jambos, most of which had already grown into trees and were affording their young master fruit and shade. His industrious hand had brought fecundity even to the most arid parts of the enclosure. Various species of aloes – some with racket-shaped leaves heavy with yellow flowers splashed with red, others like tall, spiny candles – grew on the black tops of the rocks, from which they rose as if trying to reach the long creepers covered with blue or scarlet flowers which hung here and there along the steep slopes of the mountain.

He had arranged the trees and plants so as to compose a view that could be enjoyed all at once. In the middle of the valley he had planted grasses of low growth, then shrubs, next trees of medium height and finally, around the circumference, tall trees; so that, from its centre, this vast enclosure appeared an amphitheatre of greenery, fruits and flowers, containing vegetables, strips of meadow and fields of rice and corn. But in disposing these plants and trees according to his own plan he had not strayed from Nature's; with her as his guide, he had put in the high places those whose seeds are dispersed by the wind, and beside water those with seeds designed to float : so did each plant grow in its proper site and each site receive from its plant its natural ornament. At the bottom of the valley, the streams that run down from the summit of these high rocks formed small pools in some places and in others broad mirrors which, amidst the greenery, reflected the flowering trees, the rocks and the azure of the skies.

Despite the great unevenness of the ground, most of these plantations were as accessible to the hand as to the eye. We had all provided him with help and advice to complete the work. He had cleared a path that wound round the valley and had several branches that made their way from the perimeter to the centre. Even the most rugged spots had been made to serve some purpose, and he had brought about a most harmonious union between ease of walking and roughness of ground, domestic trees and wild ones. With some of the enormous quantity of loose stones which cover most of the ground on the island and which now impede the passage along these roads, he had, here and there, fashioned pyramids in whose foundations he had put some earth together with the roots of rose-bushes, poincianas and other shrubs that prefer rocky soil, so that after a little while these rough, dark heaps were covered with greenery or with the brilliant colours of the loveliest flowers. Ravines shaded by old trees overhanging their edges formed vaulted chambers below ground where the heat never penetrated and where one could go during the day to enjoy the cool. One path led to a grove of wild trees, in the centre of which, sheltered from the wind, grew a fruit-tree laden with produce. Here was an orchard; there a field of corn ripe for the harvest. From this avenue you could see the houses; from that one the inaccessible summits of the mountain. Within a dense copse of tacamahac-trees intertwined with thick creepers not a single object could be made out at high noon, while, close by, the point of that outcrop of rock commanded a view of the entire valley and the distant sea, where sometimes a vessel would appear bound for or returning from Europe. It was on this rock that the families gathered at dusk, to enjoy in silence the coolness of the air, the perfume of the flowers, the murmur of the fountains and the final harmonies of light and shade.

Nothing could be more agreeable than the names they had given to most of the charming retreats to be found among these labyrinthine ways. The rock I have just spoken of, from which they could

see me coming at a great distance, was called 'Friendship's View'.
As soon as they caught sight of me, Paul and Virginia would signal
my arrival by running a little white handkerchief to the top of a
bamboo-cane they had once planted there in their play, just as a
flag is raised on the neighbouring mountain when a vessel is sighted
at sea. I took a fancy to carve an inscription on the stem of this tall
reed. In the course of my travels I have seen many ancient statues
and monuments, but whatever pleasure I experienced in looking at
them does not compare with that of reading a well-conceived inscription. For from these ancient stones a human voice seems to
speak across the centuries, saying to man, in the midst of deserts,
that he is not alone, that in these same places other men have
thought, felt and suffered like him : and if the inscription is the
work of some nation of antiquity which no longer exists, it opens to
the soul the realms of the infinite and, by showing that a thought
has survived the ruins even of an empire, impresses it with a sense
of its own immortality.

Thus it was that I wrote on Paul's and Virginia's little flagstaff
these verses from Horace :

> . . . *Fratres Helenae, lucida sidera,*
> *Ventorumque regat pater,*
> *Obstrictis aliis, praeter iapyga.*

'May Helen's brothers, those stars that charm like you, and the
father of the winds direct your course and make only the zephyr
blow.'

On the bark of a tacamahac-tree in whose shade Paul would
sometimes sit to gaze into the distance at the tossing sea, I carved
this line from Virgil :

> *Fortunatus et ille deos qui novit agrestes!*

'Happy, my son, to know only the rustic deities!'

And above the door of Madame de la Tour's cabin, where the
families so often met, I put this one :

At secura quies, et nescia fallere vita.

'Here is a clear conscience and a life that knows no deceit.'

But my Latin did not meet with Virginia's approval; she said
that what I had written at the base of her weather-vane was too
long and too learned, and she added : 'I should have preferred :
Shaken always, but constant.' 'A motto that would be even more
fitting if applied to virtue,' I replied. She blushed at this reflection.

The tender hearts of these happy families went out to all that
surrounded them. They had given the fondest names to things of
the most indifferent appearance. A ring of orange-, banana- and
jambo-trees, encircling a green where Paul and Virginia sometimes
went to dance, was named 'Concord'. An old tree in whose shade
Madame de la Tour and Marguerite had recounted their misfortunes was called 'Tears Wiped Away'. Some small plots of
ground where they had planted corn, peas and strawberries bore
the names 'Brittany' and 'Normandy'. Following the example of
their mistresses, and wishing to recall their birthplaces in Africa,
Domingue and Marie gave the names 'Angola' and 'Foullepointe'
to two spots that provided the grass they wove into baskets and
where they had planted a calabash-tree. These products of their
native climates helped the two expatriate families to maintain the
sweet illusion of their own countries and to soothe their longings
for home in a foreign land. Alas ! I have seen a thousand charming
titles bring to life the trees, the springs and the rocks of this valley
where confusion now reigns, and where, like some field in Greece,
all that remains is ruins and touching names.

But there was no more agreeable spot in the entire valley than
the one they called 'Virginia's Rest'. At the foot of the rock known
as 'Friendship's View' there is a hollow from which a spring rises to
form a little pool of water in the middle of a meadow of fine grass.
When Marguerite had brought Paul into the world I made her a
present of a coconut from the Indies which had been given to
me; she planted it beside the pool, intending that the tree it produced should one day serve to mark the epoch of her son's birth.
Following her friend's example, Madame de la Tour planted

another nut there with the same intention as soon as she had given birth to Virginia. From the nuts sprang two coconut-trees, which were all the family records they possessed : one they called Paul's tree, the other Virginia's. They grew in the same proportion as the children, being somewhat unequal in height, and at the end of twelve years reached above the roofs of the cabins, intertwining their palms and letting their clusters of young coconuts hang above the surface of the pool. These two trees excepted, they had left the hollow below the rock with no ornaments but those of nature. On its damp brown slopes great tufts of maidenhair beamed like green and black stars, and bunches of hart's-tongue, hanging down like long ribbons of purplish-green, waved at the wind's pleasure. Nearby were borders of periwinkles, whose blossoms are so much like those of the red gillyflower, and pimentos, their blood-red pods more brilliant than coral. Round about, the balsam-plant with its heart-shaped leaves, and basil with the odour of cloves, gave out the sweetest perfumes. From the high cliffs creepers hung like flowing draperies, covering the rock sides with great curtains of greenery. Sea birds, attracted to these peaceful retreats, would come to spend the night. At sunset one could see the curlews and sealarks flying along the shore, whilst high in the air the black frigate and the white tropic bird, like the daystar itself, were quitting the solitudes of the Indian Ocean.

Virginia liked to rest beside this fountain which was decorated with a splendour at once wild and magnificent. She would often wash the family linen in the shade of the two coconut-trees. Sometimes she would lead her goats there to graze, and while making cheeses with their milk, would watch with delight as they browsed on the maidenhair that grew on the steep sides of the rock, or stood on a ledge high in the air, as if on a pedestal. When Paul saw that this place was a favourite of hers, he brought to it the nests of every sort of bird from the neighbouring forest. Soon the parents of these birds followed their young and settled in this new colony. From time to time Virginia would come and scatter grains of rice, maize and millet among them. As soon as she appeared, whistling blackbirds, bengalis, who warble so sweetly, and cardinals with their fiery plumage would leave their bushes; parrots as green as

emeralds would fly down from the latania-trees nearby and par-
tridges come running through the grass: all of them would rush
helter-skelter to her feet like hens. She and Paul found rapturous
enjoyment in observing their play, their feeding and their loves.

Amiable children! thus did your early days pass in innocence
and the exercise of kindness. How many times, on this very spot,
did your mothers clasp you in their arms, praising Heaven for the
consolation you were preparing for their old age and giving thanks
to see you entering life under such happy auspices? How many
times, in the shadow of these rocks, did I share your country fare,
for which no animal had paid with its life? Gourds brimming with
milk, fresh eggs, rice-cakes served on banana-leaves, baskets of
sweet-potatoes, custard-apples, mangoes, oranges, pomegranates,
bananas and pineapples provided at once the most nourishing
dishes, the gayest colours and the sweetest juices.

Their conversation was as mild and innocent as these excellent
meals. Paul often talked of his day's work and of what he had to
do on the morrow. He was always planning some improvement
that would benefit them all: the paths in one place were too rough,
the seats in another were uncomfortable; these arbours he had
recently planted were not giving enough shade; Virginia would be
more comfortable over there.

In the rainy season both masters and servants would stay indoors
and occupy themselves with the weaving of grass mats and bamboo
baskets. Rakes, axes and spades were arranged in the most perfect
order against the inside of the walls, and next to these agricultural
implements were the fruits that they had helped to produce: sacks
of rice, sheaves of corn and stalks of bananas. To this abundance
they always added refinement. Virginia, instructed by her mother
and Marguerite, made sherbets and cordials from the juice of
sugar-cane, lemons and citrons.

When darkness fell, they took supper by lamplight; then
Madame de la Tour or Marguerite would tell stories of travellers
who had lost their way by night in the thief-infested woods of
Europe, or of the wreck of some vessel driven upon the rocks of a
desert island by the tempest. The tender hearts of the children
were fired with pity by these tales, and they prayed Heaven that

they might one day be allowed to show hospitality to such unfortunate people. Afterwards the two families retired separately to
rest, impatient to see each other again on the morrow. Sometimes
they fell asleep to the noise of the rain falling in torrents on the
roofs of their cabins, or to the sound of the winds that brought the
far-off murmur of waves breaking on the shore. The awareness of
distant danger only redoubled their sense of their own safety, and
they praised God for it.

From time to time Madame de la Tour would read aloud some
touching story from the Old or the New Testament. They reasoned
hardly at all upon these sacred books. Their theology was that of
Nature, consisting entirely of feeling; their morality, like that of the
Gospel, was all in their actions. They did not set aside certain days
for pleasure and others for sadness. For them each day was a feast-
day and all that surrounded them a holy temple where they admired unceasingly an Intelligence that is infinite, all-powerful and
the friend of mankind. This feeling of confidence in the Supreme
Power filled them with consolation for the past, courage for the
present and hope for the future. So it was that these two women,
compelled by misfortune to return to Nature, had developed in
themselves and in their children the feelings that Nature gives to
keep us from falling into misfortune.

But as clouds will sometimes arise to darken even the most
perfectly regulated soul, when any member of their little society
showed signs of dejection, all the others would gather round and,
rather by feelings than by reasons, put his bitter thoughts to flight.
Each of them brought his own particular qualities to the task:
Marguerite, a sprightly cheerfulness; Madame de la Tour, her
mild theology; Virginia, tender demonstrations of affection; Paul,
frankness and cordiality; even Marie and Domingue would lend
their aid. All would grieve if they saw one grieving, and weep if
they saw him weep. So do delicate plants twine together to with-
stand the hurricane.

Every Sunday in the dry season they went to mass in the church
at Pamplemousses, whose steeple you can see over there on the
plain. On several occasions rich settlers, who arrived in palanquins,
showed themselves eager to make the acquaintance of two such

united families and to invite them to share their amusements. But they always declined these offers with civility and respect; for they were persuaded that the powerful look only for complaisance in the weak and that one can only be complaisant to others by flattering their passions, whether good or bad. On the other hand, they were no less careful to avoid familiarity with the poorer class of settlers, who were commonly jealous, rude and backbiting. At first one group supposed them diffident and the other proud; but their conduct, though reserved, was accompanied by such obliging marks of politeness, especially towards those most in need, that, by imperceptible degrees, they gained the respect of the rich and the confidence of the poor.

When mass was over they often found that their good offices were required. A person stricken with grief might seek their advice, or a child come with a request to visit its mother who was lying ill in one of the nearby districts. They always carried with them a few remedies for the illnesses that were common among the settlers, to which they added the ready goodwill that gives such value to small favours. They were especially successful in driving away those torments of the mind that are so intolerable when one is alone or infirm of body. Madame de la Tour spoke with such confidence of the Divinity that the sick could feel His presence as they listened to her. Virginia's eyes were often wet with tears as she returned from these visits, but her heart was full of joy at having had the opportunity to do good. It was she who prepared in advance the medicines they would require and, with ineffable grace, distributed them to those who were ill.

After these acts of humanity, they sometimes went on through the valley of the Long Mountain as far as my house, where I used to prepare dinner for them on the banks of the little river that flows through my neighbourhood. For these occasions I would procure a few bottles of old wine, increasing the cheer of our Indian meals with these pleasant and cordial productions of Europe. At other times we would arrange to meet on the shore at a spot where some small rivers, which here are little more than large streams, flowed into the sea. We brought with us fruit and vegetables from our gardens, and to these we added what the sea furnished in abundance : polyps, bullheads, red mullet, crayfish, shrimps and crabs, which we caught along the shore, as well as sea-urchins, oysters and every sort of shellfish. The most terrible sites often yielded the serenest enjoyment. Sometimes, seated on a rock in the shade of a velvet-tree, we would watch the waves sweep in from the open sea and break at our feet with a horrible crash. Paul, who could swim like a fish, liked to go out on the reefs to meet the breakers; as they drew near he would flee to shore before their great roaring scrolls of foam, which pursued him well up the beach. Whenever she saw him do this, Virginia would cry out sharply, saying that games of that kind filled her with dread.

When we had finished our meal the two young people would dance and sing. Virginia's song told of the happiness of rustic life and of the disasters that befall seamen who sail for gain upon that furious element instead of tilling the earth, peaceful giver of so much that is good. Sometimes she would perform a mime with Paul in the native fashion. Mime is the first language of man and is known in all countries; it is so natural and expressive that the children of the white settlers lose no time in learning it themselves once they have seen it practised by the black children of the island. Recalling the stories that had most affected her in her mother's reading, Virginia reproduced the main incidents with great naturalness and simplicity. To the sound of Domingue's tom-tom, she would appear on the greensward carrying a pitcher on her head and timidly approach a nearby spring to draw water. Domingue and Marie, representing the shepherds of Midian, would forbid her to come near and pretend to drive her away. Paul would rush to help her, drive off the shepherds and fill her pitcher; placing it on her head he would crown her with a garland of red periwinkle blossoms which set off her fair complexion. Then, joining in their game, I would take the character of Reuel and give Paul my daughter Zipporah in marriage.

Another time she took the part of the unfortunate Ruth returning widowed and poor to her own country, where, after a long absence, she finds herself a stranger. Domingue and Marie played the reapers. Virginia followed their steps, pretending to glean here and there a few ears of corn. Assuming the gravity of a patriarch,

Paul put questions to her; trembling, she replied to them. His compassion was soon aroused and he granted hospitality to innocence and refuge to adversity; filling Virginia's apron with provisions of every kind, he led her before us as before the elders of the city, declaring that he was taking her for his wife in spite of her poverty. Madame de la Tour, reminded by this scene of her abandonment by her own family, her widowhood, the kind reception Marguerite had given her and their present hopes for a happy marriage between their children, could not refrain from weeping; and this confused memory of happiness and woe made us all shed tears of mingled joy and sorrow.

So lifelike was the presentation of these stories that we felt as if we had been transported to the fields of Syria or Palestine. Nor did our plays want for suitable scenery, lighting and music. The stage was usually set at a cross-roads in the forest, where the openings between the trees formed leafy arcades around us, and in the centre of which we were sheltered from the heat all day. When the sun had sunk on the horizon, its rays, broken by the trunks of the trees, glanced in long sheaves of light into the shadows of the forest to produce the most majestic effects. Sometimes the whole of its fiery disc appeared at the end of an avenue and made it sparkle with light. Then the foliage of the trees, illuminated from below by the saffron rays, glowed with the fire of the emerald and the topaz; their brown and mossy trunks seemed to be transformed into columns of antique bronze; and the birds, who had already retired for the night beneath the dark leaves, surprised to see a second dawn, broke silence all together, greeting the daystar with thousands upon thousands of songs.

Very often, during these rustic entertainments, darkness would come upon us unawares, but the mildness of the climate and the purity of the air were such that we could pass the night in the forest under an *ajoupa*, and we had no fear of thieves either close at hand or far away. Each of us would return home next day to find his cabin as he had left it. At that time, before the growth of trade, there was such integrity and simple honesty on the island that the doors of many houses had neither lock nor key; indeed for a number of Creoles a lock was an object of curiosity.

There were, however, two days in the year that were occasions of special rejoicing for Paul and Virginia: their mothers' name-days. The evening before, Virginia would be sure to knead some flour and bake wheaten cakes, which she would send to poor white families who, having been born on the island, had never tasted European bread, and who, without any blacks to help them and reduced to living in the woods on cassava roots, had neither the dullness that goes with slavery nor the courage that comes from education to help make their poverty bearable. These cakes were the only presents that could be made out of the meagre surplus of the settlement, but she gave them with such good grace that they were highly prized. Paul was given the task of carrying them to the poor families who, as they accepted them, would agree to come and spend the next day with Madame de la Tour and Marguerite.

On the morrow, a mother would arrive with two or three wretched daughters, thin, sallow and so fearful that they dared not lift their eyes from the ground. Virginia soon put them at ease. To enhance the goodness of the refreshments she served, and to make the occasion more agreeable, she would relate some parti-cular circumstance of each. Marguerite had prepared this drink; her mother had prepared that one; her brother had picked this fruit himself from the top of a tree. She would urge Paul to invite them to dance. Until she saw that they had all they wanted and were content, she would not leave them, for she wished them to share the joy of her family. 'One can only find happiness,' she would say, 'by making others happy.' When they were ready to leave she would press them to accept anything that seemed to have given them pleasure, insisting on the novelty and originality of her presents to conceal the fact that they were in need of what she gave. If she noticed that their clothes were unusually tattered, she would obtain her mother's consent to choose some of her own and send Paul to leave them secretly at the door of their cabin. She thus performed her good actions after the example of the Divinity: concealing the benefactor, revealing only the benefit.

You Europeans, whose minds are filled from childhood with so many prejudices that make against happiness, cannot conceive that such understanding and such pleasure can be given by Nature.

Confined within a narrow sphere of human learning, your souls
soon reach the limits of their artificial enjoyments, whilst Nature
and the heart are inexhaustible. Paul and Virginia had no clocks
or almanacks, no books of chronology, history or philosophy.
They regulated their lives according to the cycles of Nature. They
knew the hours of the day by the shadows of the trees, the seasons
by the times when they flower or fruit, and the years by the number
of their crops. As a result, the most delightful images were scattered
through their conversations. 'It is dinner-time,' Virginia would
say to the family, 'the shadows of the banana-trees are at their
feet;' or, 'Night will fall soon, the tamarinds are closing their
leaves.'

'When will you come and see us?' some girls who lived nearby
would ask. 'At sugar-cane time,' she would answer, and her friends
would reply : 'Your visit will be all the sweeter and more pleasant.'

When she was asked about her age and Paul's she would say :
'My brother is as old as the big coconut-tree beside the pool and I
am as old as the small one. The mango-trees have given their
fruit twelve times and the orange-trees their blossoms twenty-four
times since I came into the world.' Like fauns and dryads, their
existence seemed to be linked to that of the trees. They knew no
history but the events of their mothers' lives, no chronology but
that of their orchards and no philosophy but to do good to others
and to resign themselves to the will of God.

After all, what need had these young people of the riches and
learning that we prize so highly? Their want and their ignorance
only added to their felicity. Not a day passed without their giving
each other some help or some enlightenment – yes, enlightenment;
and if their talk sometimes contained errors, what danger have
these for the man whose life is pure? Thus did they grow, these
two children of Nature. No cares had furrowed their brows, no
intemperance had corrupted their blood, no unhappy passion had
depraved their hearts : each day innocence, piety and love unfolded the beauty of their souls which shone in the ineffable grace
of their features, their carriage and their movements. They were in
the morning of life and had all its freshness : so must our first
parents have appeared in the garden of Eden when, coming from

the hands of God, they saw each other and drew near and talked
for the first time as brother and sister; Virginia, modest, trusting
and mild like Eve, and Paul, another Adam, having the stature of a
man and the simplicity of a child.

He must have told me a thousand times how, finding himself
alone with her sometimes on his return from work, he would say:
'The sight of you restores me when I am weary. When, from high
on the mountain, I see you on the floor of the valley, you appear
to me in the midst of our orchards like a rosebud. The partridge
that runs towards her little ones has not so graceful a form or so
light a step as you when you walk towards our mothers' houses.
Although the trees should hide you from my sight, I have no need
to see you to find you again; something of you that I cannot express
remains for me in the air when you pass, on the grass where you
rest. When I come near you, all my senses are ravished. The azure
of the heavens is not so lovely as the blue of your eyes, nor the
song of the bengalis so sweet as the sound of your voice. If I touch
you with only the tip of my finger, my whole body thrills with
pleasure. Do you remember the day we crossed the slippery stones
of the river of the Three Paps? I was already very tired when we
reached the bank, but when I had taken you on my back I seemed
to be winged like a bird. Tell me which of your charms it was that
enchanted me. It cannot be your understanding, for our mothers
have more than the two of us. Nor your caresses, for they embrace
me more often than you. I think it must be your goodness. I shall
never forget that you walked barefoot as far as the Black River
to ask pardon for a poor runaway slave. Here, my beloved, take
this branch of lemon-flowers that I've brought from the forest and
keep it by your bed at night. Eat this honeycomb which I took
from the top of a high rock for you. But first lay your head on my
breast and I shall be weary no longer.'

Virginia would reply: 'Oh my brother, your presence gives me
more joy than the rays of the morning sun on the pinnacles of
these rocks. I love both our mothers well, but when they call you
"my son" I love them still more. I feel the caresses they give you
more than those that I receive myself. You ask why you love me:
but those that have been brought up together always love each

other. Look at our birds: they were reared in the same nest, they love each other as we do and like us they are always together. Listen to them calling and answering each other from tree to tree: so do I repeat the words of the airs that you play on your flute high on the mountain when the echo carries them to me in the valley below. You were always dear to me, but especially so since the day you wanted to fight the slave's master for my sake. Since that time I have often said to myself: "Ah! my brother has a good heart; but for him, I should have died of fright." I pray to God every day for my mother and yours, for you and for our poor servants, but I seem to grow more devout when I pronounce your name. How I entreat God that no harm may come to you! Why do you go so far and climb so high to bring me fruit and flowers? Have we not enough in the garden? How tired you seem! And you are all bathed in sweat.' And with her little white handkerchief she would wipe his brow and his cheeks and give him many kisses.

Yet for some time Virginia had been troubled by a strange ailment. Her skin took on a yellow tint; her fine blue eyes became shot with black; all her body felt languid and oppressed. Serenity was gone from her brow, the smile from her lips. She would suddenly assume a joyless gaiety or appear dejected without cause. She fled her innocent games, her easy tasks, the company of her beloved family to wander here and there in the loneliest parts of the settlement, seeking respite everywhere but finding it nowhere. Sometimes, at the sight of Paul, she would run playfully towards him; then, having nearly reached her goal, she would stop, seized with a sudden embarrassment; her pale cheeks would flush deeply and her eyes no longer dare to rest on his. Paul would say to her: 'The rocks are covered with greenery, the birds sing when you come into sight; all around you is gay, you alone are sad.' And he would seek to revive her spirits with a kiss; but she would turn her head away and run trembling to her mother. Her brother's caresses threw the unhappy girl into confusion. Paul was at a loss to understand such strange and unusual shifts of mood.

Misfortunes seldom come alone. One of those summers which now and again devastate the lands lying between the tropics had arrived to ravage the Ile de France. It was near the end of Decem-

ber when the vertical fires of the sun in Capricorn beat down upon
the island for three weeks and set it ablaze. The south-east wind,
which blows for most of the year, had ceased. Long swirls of dust
rose from the roads and hung suspended in the air. The grass was
burnt, most of the streams had dried up; everywhere cracks opened
in the earth and hot vapours rose from the sides of the mountains.
Not a single cloud came in from the sea. Only reddish-brown mists
arose from its calm surface during the day and appeared like the
flames of a conflagration in the rays of the setting sun. Even the
night could not cool the sweltering atmosphere. The orb of the
moon rose immense and red on a horizon veiled in haze. The ex-
hausted herds lay down on the hillsides and, craning their necks
towards the sky to seek a breath of air, made the valleys resound
with their melancholy lowing. Even the Caffre who led them tried
to cool himself by stretching out on the ground; but everywhere
the earth was scorching and the stifling air hummed with the sound
of insects seeking to quench their thirst with the blood of men and
animals.

During one of these burning nights, Virginia felt all the symp-
toms of her malady return with redoubled force. Several times she
got up, sat down, then returned to bed, but in none of these
positions could she find either sleep or rest. By the light of the moon
she turns her steps towards her fountain; she can see the stream
which, despite the drought, continues to trickle in silver threads
over the brown sides of the rock. She plunges into her pool. The
first shock of cool water revives her spirits and a thousand pleasant
memories come to her mind. She remembers that her mother and
Marguerite enjoyed bathing her with Paul in this very place when
they were children; but that later Paul, intending to reserve it for
her alone, had dug out the basin, covered the bottom with sand
and planted sweet-smelling herbs on its banks. She can make out
in the dim water, on her bare arms and on her breast, the reflection
of the two palm-trees that were planted at her brother's birth and
at her own, intertwining their green branches and their young
coconuts above her head. She thinks of Paul's affection, softer than
the scent of blossom, purer than spring water, stronger than palm-
trees joined together; and she sighs. Her thoughts turn to the night

and to solitude, and suddenly she is possessed with a consuming fire. Filled with fear by these dangerous shadows and by these waters that burn hotter than the sun in the torrid zone, she leaves the pool and hurries to her mother's side to seek support in this struggle with herself. Several times, wishing to reveal her sufferings, she presses her hands in her own; more than once she is about to speak Paul's name, but her overburdened heart deprives her tongue of utterance and, laying her head on her mother's bosom, she can only give way to a flood of tears.

Madame de la Tour discerned well enough the cause of her daughter's distress, but she dared not speak of it with her. 'My child,' she said, 'you must look to God for help. He bestows health and life at His pleasure. He is trying you today only to reward you tomorrow. Remember that we have been put on earth for no other reason than to practise virtue.'

About this time the excessive heat drew up from the ocean vapours which hung over the island like a vast parasol, and gathered round the mountain-tops, whose mist-enshrouded peaks now and again sent forth long streaks of fire. Soon the woods, the plains and the valleys resounded with frightful bursts of thunder and the rains fell like dreadful cataracts from the sky. Foaming torrents rushed down the sides of the mountain; the floor of the valley became a sea, the plateau where the cabins stood a little island, and the entrance to the valley a sluice through which earth, trees and rocks were carried pell-mell by the roaring waters.

The trembling families gathered in Madame de la Tour's cabin to pray, while the roof cracked horribly under the buffeting of the winds. Although the doors and windows were securely fastened, every object around could clearly be made out through the joints of the framework, so vivid and frequent was the lightning. Despite the raging of the tempest, Paul, followed by Domingue, went fearlessly from one cabin to the other, here strengthening a wall with a buttress, there driving in a stake, coming in only to console the family with the hope that fair weather would soon return. And indeed by evening the rain had ceased; the south-east trade wind began to blow again as usual; the storm clouds were driven towards the north-west and the setting sun appeared on the horizon.

Virginia's first wish was to see how her resting-place had fared. Paul approached her timidly and offered his arm for her to lean on as she walked. She accepted it with a smile and together they stepped out of the cabin into the cool and resonant air. Clouds of white mist rose from the rounded crests of the mountain; here and there its slopes were furrowed by the foaming torrents which were now diminishing on all sides. As for the garden, it was completely devastated; dreadful gullies scored its surface; most of the fruit-trees had been uprooted; great piles of sand covered the borders of the meadows and had filled in the basin of Virginia's pool. The two coconut-trees still stood in their places, green and flourishing, but round about them not a lawn nor a bower nor a bird remained – except for a few bengalis which, from nearby points of rock, bewailed the loss of their little ones in plaintive song.

At the sight of this devastation, Virginia said to Paul: 'You brought birds to this place; the hurricane has killed them. You planted this garden; it has been destroyed. Everything on earth perishes; in heaven alone is there no change.'

'If only I could give you something from heaven,' replied Paul, 'but I have no possessions, not even earthly ones.'

'You do have one,' returned Virginia blushing, 'the portrait of Saint Paul.'

She had hardly spoken these words when he ran to his mother's cabin to fetch it. The portrait was a tiny miniature of Paul the Hermit, to whom Marguerite was greatly devoted. As a girl she had long worn it round her neck, and when she became a mother she had put it round her child's. It had even come about that, when she was pregnant with Paul and had been deserted by family and friends, by dint of contemplating the image of this blessed recluse the baby in her womb had acquired some resemblance to it; and this had decided her (she who had been wronged and then abandoned) to give her child the name and the protection of a saint who had passed his life far from mankind. As she accepted the little portrait from Paul's hands, Virginia said in a voice touched with emotion: 'Dear brother, it shall never be removed from me as long as I live, and I shall never forget that you gave me the only thing in the world that you possessed.' Her affectionate tone, and this unhoped-for return of intimacy and tenderness, encouraged Paul to try to embrace her but, light as a bird, she escaped, leaving him astonished and with no idea what this extraordinary behaviour could mean.

Things had developed so far when Marguerite said to Madame de la Tour: 'Why do we not marry our children? Their passion for one another is extreme. My son may be unaware of it now but when once Nature has spoken to him, watching over them will be vain; the worst is to be feared.'

'They are too young and too poor,' Madame de la Tour replied. 'Imagine our grief if Virginia were to bring wretched children into the world which she would perhaps not have the strength to bring up. Your Negro Domingue is old and worn out, Marie is frail; for the last fifteen years, dear friend, I have felt much weakened myself. One grows old rapidly in warm countries and more quickly still in affliction. Paul is our only hope. Let us wait until age has developed his character and he is able to support us by his labour. At present, as you know, we have only the bare necessity for each day. But if we send Paul to India for a short time he can earn enough by trading to buy a slave, and on his return home we will marry him to Virginia; for I believe that no one can make my beloved daughter as happy as your son. We will consult our neighbour.'

The two ladies did seek my advice and I gave my approval to their plan. 'The Indian Ocean is calm,' I told them. 'The crossing from here to India in a favourable season takes no more than six weeks at most, and as much for the return voyage. We will collect some merchandise for Paul in our district, for some of my neighbours are very fond of him. We need only provide him with raw cotton which we make no use of for want of mills to dress it; ebony, so common here that it serves for firewood, and some resins that go to waste in our woods; these things sell quite well in the Indies and are altogether useless to us here.'

I took it upon myself to ask Monsieur de la Bourdonnais' permission for Paul to embark, but above all I wanted to acquaint the young man with our plans for the voyage. Imagine my astonishment, however, when he said to me with a degree of good sense far beyond his years: 'Why do you want me to leave my family for this doubtful venture? Is any commerce in the world more profitable than tilling a field, which sometimes returns fifty- and a hundred-fold on your labour? If we want to trade, can we not take our surplus to the town to sell without my running off to the Indies? Our mothers tell me that Domingue has grown old and weak, but I am young and growing stronger each day. What if an accident should happen while I was away, especially to Virginia who is already unwell? No, no! I cannot make up my mind to leave them.'

His reply threw me into great confusion, for Madame de la Tour had made no secret to me of the state of Virginia's feelings or of her wish to put some distance between the two young people until they should have grown a few years older. But I could say nothing that might lead Paul to suspect these motives.

While these discussions were going on a vessel arrived from France with a letter for Madame de la Tour from her aunt. A grave illness had left the old woman in a state of increasing debility which was incurable at her age; and fear of death, which alone can soften the hardest hearts, had seized her. She summoned her niece to return to France; or, if her health would not permit her to make such a long voyage, she enjoined her to send Virginia in her place. She would see to it that her daughter received a good education and a place at court, and she would settle her entire estate upon her. The renewal of her favours, she added, was conditional upon her orders being obeyed.

The letter was no sooner read than it spread consternation through the family. Marie and Domingue began to weep. Paul, motionless with astonishment, seemed ready to fly into a rage, while Virginia fixed her eyes on her mother without daring to utter a word.

'Could you leave us now?' asked Marguerite.

'No, my dear friend; no, my children,' returned Madame de la Tour: 'I shall not leave you. I have lived with you and it is with you that I want to die. I have found happiness nowhere but in your affection. If my health is unsettled, it is my former sorrows that are to blame. The harshness of my relations and the loss of my dear husband wounded me to the heart. But since then I have found more consolation and real happiness with you, in these poor cabins, than ever the riches of my family allowed me even to hope for in my native country.'

At these words tears of joy fell from every eye. 'Nor shall I leave you,' said Paul, pressing Madame de la Tour in his arms; 'I will not go to the Indies. With all of us to work for you, dear Mother, you will never want for anything.' But of them all it was Virginia who was most keenly touched, although she showed her joy the least. For the rest of the day her manner was one of subdued cheerfulness, and the return of her tranquillity completed the general satisfaction.

The next day at sunrise, they had just completed the morning prayer that they always made together before breakfast when Domingue announced that a gentleman on horseback was approaching the settlement, followed by two slaves. The gentleman was Monsieur de la Bourdonnais. When he entered the cabin, where the family was seated at table, Virginia had just served the coffee and boiled rice that is the usual breakfast on the island, to which she had added hot sweet-potatoes and fresh bananas. Halved gourds were all they had for dishes and banana-leaves for table-linen. The governor first expressed some surprise at the poverty of their dwelling; then, addressing Madame de la Tour, he said that the general duties of his office sometimes prevented him from concerning himself with individuals but that she had every right to his special consideration. 'Madame,' he went on, 'you have a noble and very wealthy aunt who intends to leave her fortune to you, and who expects you to come to her in Paris.' Madame de la Tour replied that her poor health would not permit her to undertake such a long voyage. 'Then at least think of Mademoiselle de la Tour,' returned the governor, 'it would be unjust of you to deprive so young and so amiable a daughter of so great an inheritance. I will not conceal from you that your aunt has used her influence with the authorities to bring your daughter to France. I have received a letter about the matter instructing me to use the powers of my office if necessary; but as I choose to exercise them only for the happiness of those who live in the colony, I trust that you will of your own accord consent to the sacrifice of a few years for the sake of your daughter's establishment and your own well-being for the rest of your life. Why do people come to the islands if not to make a fortune? Is it not far more agreeable to return to one's native country and find it there?'

As he said these words, he took a great sack of piastres from one of his Negroes and placed it on the table. 'Your aunt has sent this,' he continued, 'to provide whatever is necessary for the young lady's voyage.' He concluded by gently reproaching Madame de la Tour for not having applied to him in her need, at the same time praising the noble courage she had shown.

Paul spoke up immediately : 'But my mother did apply to you, Monsieur,' he said to the governor, 'and you received her very badly.'

'Have you another child, Madame?' asked Monsieur de la Bourdonnais.

'No, Monsieur,' she replied, 'he is my friend's son; but we are parents to him and to Virginia alike and they are equally dear to us.'

'Young man,' said the governor to Paul, 'when you have acquired some experience of the world, you will understand the misfortune of those in authority; you will realize how easily they can be influenced and how readily they give to scheming vice what belongs to hidden merit.'

At Madame de la Tour's invitation, Monsieur de la Bourdonnais took the place next to hers at the table and breakfasted in the Creole fashion on coffee mixed with boiled rice. He was much taken with the order and cleanliness of the little cabin, the unity of these two charming families and the eagerness with which their old servants attended them. 'There may be no more than simple wooden furniture here,' he said, 'but there are serene faces and hearts of gold.' Paul was enchanted by the governor's affability. 'I wish to be your friend,' said he, 'for you are an honest man.' Monsieur de la Bourdonnais received this mark of insular cordiality with pleasure; he shook Paul's hand and embraced him, and assured him that he could rely upon his friendship.

After breakfast he took Madame de la Tour aside and told her that there would soon be an opportunity to send her daughter to France on a vessel which was ready to set sail; that among the passengers was a lady who was a relation of his and in whose protection he would put Virginia; and that she must take care not to give up an immense fortune for the sake of a few years' contentment. He added as he was leaving : 'I have received letters from friends of your aunt assuring me that she cannot last more than two years. Think the matter over carefully. Fortune doesn't come every day. Discuss it with your family. Every person of good sense will advise you as I do.' She replied that as she now desired no other happiness in the world but her daughter's, she would leave the question of her departure for France entirely to her own decision.

Madame de la Tour was not sorry to have found an occasion to separate Virginia and Paul for a time in the interests of their future happiness together. Taking her daughter aside, she said to her : 'My child, our servants are old; Paul is very young; Marguerite is nearing old age, and I am already much weakened in health. If I were to die and leave you without fortune, what would become of you in this wilderness? You would be left all alone with no one who could be of great help to you and would be forced to gain your livelihood by unceasing work on the land like a hired labourer. The thought of it cuts me to the heart.'

'But it is God who has condemned us to labour,' replied Virginia; 'and you have taught me to work and to bless Him each day. He has never forsaken us before and He will not forsake us now. His providence watches particularly over the unfortunate. How many times have you told me so yourself, Mother? No; I cannot make up my mind to leave you.'

Madame de la Tour was touched. 'My only desire is to make you happy,' she returned, 'and one day to marry you to Paul, who is not really your brother. Remember that his fortune too depends on your decision.'

When a girl is in love she thinks that no one is aware of it but her. She covers her eyes with the veil that she keeps on her heart; but when it is lifted by a friendly hand, then love's hidden sorrows escape as through an open gate and the tender effusions of confi-

1. The Childhood of Paul and Virginia

Peint par A.L.Girodet   Gravé par B. Roger

2. Crossing the Torrent

3. The Bird's Nest

4. Malabar Women Washing Virginia's Body

dence replace the reserve and mystery in which she had wrapped
herself. Virginia, alive to these new proofs of her mother's goodness, told her of the struggles she had undergone with God as her
only witness; that she recognized His providence in the help of a
loving mother who approved of her attachment and who would
guide her by advice; and that now, strengthened by her support,
there was every reason to remain at her side without anxiety for the
present or fear for the future.

Madame de la Tour saw that her confidence had produced an
effect quite the opposite of the one she had expected. 'My child,'
she said, 'I have no wish to make you act against your will. Take
time to think; but hide your love from Paul. When a girl's heart
is engaged, there is no more that her lover can ask of her.'

Towards evening, when she and Virginia were alone, a tall priest
dressed in a blue cassock entered the cabin. A missionary on the
island, he was the confessor of both Madame de la Tour and her
daughter. The governor had sent him. 'God be praised, my children,' said he as he came in; 'now that you are rich, you can heed
the promptings of your good hearts and help the poor. I know what
Monsieur de la Bourdonnais told you and the answer that you
gave him. Good mother, you are obliged to remain here because of
your health; but you, young lady, have no excuse. We must be
obedient to Providence and to our older relations, even when they
make unjust demands of us. It is a sacrifice, but it is God's command. He offered Himself for us and we must follow His example
and sacrifice ourselves when the good of our family is at stake. Your
journey to France will end happily. You will surely consent to go,
my dear young lady?'

Trembling and with downcast eyes, Virginia replied: 'If it is
God's command, I cannot oppose it. God's will be done!' she said
through her tears.

When the missionary had gone to give the governor an account
of the success of his errand, Madame de la Tour sent Domingue
to ask me to come to the settlement to advise her about Virginia's
departure. My opinion was absolutely against her being allowed to
go. I consider that happiness depends upon two certain principles:
that we should hold the advantages of Nature above those of

fortune, and that we should never seek outside ourselves what we can find within. These maxims I apply to everything without exception. But what weight could my arguments for moderation have against the illusions of a great fortune or my natural reasons against the prejudices of the world and an authority that was sacred for Madame de la Tour? The lady consulted me only out of politeness; after her confessor's decision her mind was made up. Even Marguerite, who had strongly opposed the departure despite the advantages she hoped would come to her son from Virginia's fortune, no longer made any objection. As for Paul, unaware of the decision that was being taken and perplexed at the secret conversations between Madame de la Tour and her daughter, he gave himself up to gloomy sadness. 'They must be scheming against me,' said he, 'for why else would they hide from me?'

Meanwhile the news that fortune had visited this rocky valley had spread over the island, and merchants of every kind were soon to be seen climbing up to the settlement. Amidst these poor dwellings they unfolded the richest cloths of India : splendid dimities from Gudalur; handkerchiefs from Pulicat and from Masulipatam; plain, striped and embroidered muslins from Dacca, transparent as daylight; bafts of splendid whiteness from Surat; chintzes of every colour and of the rarest kinds, decorated with flecks and with green branches. They unrolled magnificent silken stuffs from China, lampas cut in open-work patterns; damasks that were white and satin-smooth and others of meadow-green and dazzling red; pink taffetas, rich heavy satins, pekins as soft as cloth, white and yellow nankeens, and even *pagnes* from Madagascar.

Madame de la Tour wished her daughter to buy everything that would give her pleasure but, fearing that the merchants might cheat her, she kept a wary eye on the prices and the quality of the goods. Virginia chose whatever she thought would please her mother, Marguerite and Paul. 'This would make a good covering for furniture,' she would say, or, 'Marie and Domingue could make use of that.' In this way the sack of piastres was used up before she had given a thought to her own needs, and it was necessary to return to her a share of the presents she had distributed to the others.

Paul was grief-stricken at the sight of all these gifts of fortune, which presaged the departure of Virginia. He came to my house a few days later and said with a dejected air : 'My sister is going away; she is already making preparations for her voyage. Come to our settlement, I beseech you. Use the influence you have with her mother and mine to keep her at home.' I yielded to his entreaties, although I was perfectly convinced that my representations would have no effect.

Virginia had always seemed charming to me in blue Bengal cloth and with a red handkerchief tied round her head but, arrayed like one of the ladies of this country, she made another sort of impression altogether. She was dressed in white muslin lined with pink taffeta. Her high and slender waist was perfectly outlined by her bodice, and her blonde hair, which she wore in two plaits, was an admirable ornament to her maidenly head. Her fine blue eyes were full of melancholy and the passion she was struggling against in her heart gave a flush to her complexion and to her voice tones rich with emotion. Her elegant attire, which she seemed to have put on in spite of herself, contrasted with her languishment and made it all the more affecting. It was impossible to see or hear her without being moved. Her appearance only increased Paul's sadness. Marguerite, distressed at his situation, took him aside and said, 'My son, why do you entertain false hopes which only add to the bitterness of privation ? It is time that I made known the secret of your life and mine. Mademoiselle de la Tour is related, through her mother, to a rich lady of high rank, whilst you are no more than the son of a poor countrywoman and, what is worse, you are a bastard.'

Paul was greatly astonished by the word 'bastard', which he had never heard before. He asked his mother what it meant. 'You had no legitimate father,' she replied. 'You are the offspring of a weakness that I committed for love whilst still a girl. My fault deprived you of your father's family, and my repentance of your mother's. Unhappy child ! you have no other relation in the world but me !' At this she gave way to a flood of tears.

'Oh my dear mother,' said Paul, pressing her in his arms, 'if you are my only relation in the world, then I shall love you all the more. But what a secret you have revealed! This explains why Mademoiselle de la Tour has been avoiding me for these two months and why she is now determined to leave. Ah! it is quite clear that she despises me.'

The supper-hour having arrived, we took our places at the table; but, each of us being troubled by a different emotion, we ate little and spoke not at all. Virginia was the first to get up; she went out and sat down on this very spot where we are now. Paul followed before long and sat beside her. They remained in deep silence for some time. It was one of those exquisite nights which are so frequent in the tropics and whose beauty is beyond the powers of the most accomplished painter. The moon appeared amidst the firmament, surrounded by a veil of cloud which its beams were dispersing by degrees. Its light diffused itself imperceptibly over the mountains of the island, making their peaks shine with a silvery green. The wind held its breath. From the woods, from deep in the valleys, from high on the rocks could be heard the little cries and the soft murmuring of birds caressing each other in their nests. Every creature, down to the insects chirping under the grass, rejoiced in the brightness of the night and the stillness of the air. The stars sparkled in the sky, and were reflected on the bosom of the sea, which sent back their trembling images. Virginia's eyes wandered distractedly over the vast, sombre expanse of the ocean, distinguishable from the shore of the island only by the red lights of the fishermen. At the entrance to the harbour she could make out a light and a shadow: these were the deck-lantern and the dark hull of the ship in which she was to embark for Europe. It was lying at anchor, ready to set sail when the calm should pass. The sight of it troubled her and she turned her head aside so that Paul might not see her tears.

Madame de la Tour, Marguerite and myself were seated a few paces from them under some banana-trees. I have never forgotten their conversation, which we could hear distinctly in the silence of the night.

'Mademoiselle,' said Paul, 'I am told that you are going away, in three days' time. Are you not afraid to expose yourself to the dangers of the sea . . . the sea which so frightens you?'

'I must obey the wishes of my family,' replied Virginia, 'and I must do my duty.'

'But,' returned Paul, 'you are leaving us for a distant relation whom you have never seen.'

'Alas,' said Virginia, 'I wanted to remain here all my life but it was not my mother's wish. My confessor told me that it was God's will that I should go, that life was a trial. Oh! it is a hard trial indeed!'

'What!' rejoined Paul, 'so many reasons for going away and not one to keep you here! Ah, but there must be others which you are keeping from me. Riches are very enticing. In a new world you will soon find someone to whom you can give the name of brother that you no longer give me. You will choose him from among those who are worthy of you, those who have the high birth and the fortune that I cannot offer you. But where will you find greater happiness than you have here? What land that you can reach will be dearer to you than the one where you were born? Where will you be able to bring together fonder companions than those who love you? How will you exist without your mother's caresses, to which you are so accustomed? Now that she is old, what will become of her when you are no longer at her side, at her table, in her house; when she can no longer take your arm on her walks? What will become of my mother who loves you as dearly as your own? What shall I say to them when I see them weeping because you are far away? Oh, you are cruel! I have said not a word of myself: but what will become of me when I no longer see you among us in the morning, and when night comes without bringing us together? When I see these two palm-trees planted at our birth which have so long been the witnesses of our mutual affection? Ah! since your destiny has changed, since you seek in far-away lands other possessions than those my work can provide, let me go with you on the vessel that takes you away. I will comfort you in the tempests which so frighten you on land; I will lay your head on my breast, warm your heart against my heart; and in France, where you are going in search of wealth and position, I will serve you as a slave and be content if only I can see you happy in the great houses where you will be adored and waited upon. Then

I shall be rich and noble enough at least to make the greatest of all
sacrifices by dying at your feet.'

Here sobs choked his voice. Immediately we heard Virginia
reply in these words, broken by sighs : 'It is for your sake that I am
leaving . . . for you whom I have seen each day bent in toil to provide for two helpless families. If I have taken the opportunity of
becoming rich, it is only so that I can return a thousand-fold what
you have done for us. But no fortune is worth your affection. What
is it that you said of your birth? Oh, if it were possible now to have
another brother, would I choose anyone but you? Oh Paul! Paul!
you are far more dear to me than a brother! How much it has cost
me to rebuff you. I wanted your help to keep me from my very self
until the day that Heaven could bless our union. But now I will
stay or go; I will live or die. Do with me what you will. Faint-
hearted girl that I am, I could resist your embraces, but your
suffering quite overcomes me.'

At these words Paul seized her in his arms and held her tightly,
crying out in a terrible voice : 'I am going to France with her;
nothing can part me from her.' We all ran to him. 'My son,' said
Madame de la Tour, 'if you leave, what will become of us?'

Trembling, he repeated her words : 'My son, my son' . . . then,
'How can you be my mother,' said he, 'when you separate brother
from sister? You nourished both of us with your milk; you reared
us on your knee and taught us to love each other; we have said so a
thousand times. And now you are taking her from me. You are
sending her to Europe, to the barbarous country that refused to
grant you refuge and to the cruel relations who abandoned you
in your need. You will say that I have no rights over her, that she
is not my sister. But she is everything to me : birth, family, riches,
everything that is good. I know no other. We have lived under the
same roof and shared the same cradle and we shall lie in the same
tomb. If she goes, I must follow her. Who will prevent me? The
governor? Can he prevent me from throwing myself into the sea,
from swimming after her? The sea cannot be more fatal to me
now than the land. If I cannot live near her here, I can at least die
in her sight, far from you. Inhuman mother! Pitiless woman! May
the ocean to which you expose her never return her to you; may

the waves carry back my body and roll it with hers among the pebbles of the shore, and so give you, in the loss of your two children, eternal cause for grief.'

At these words I seized him in my arms, for despair was depriving him of his reason. His eyes flashed, great drops of sweat streamed down his flaming countenance, his knees shook, and in his burning breast I could feel his heart beating with redoubled force.

Virginia was frightened. 'Oh, my dear,' she said, 'I solemnly affirm by the pleasures of our early years, by your pains and mine and by all that must attach forever two unfortunate beings that, if I stay, I will live only for you, and, if I go, I will return one day to be yours. I call you to witness, all you who raised me as a child, who may dispose of my life as you please and who see the tears that I now shed. I swear it by the Heaven that hears me, by the sea that I must cross and the air that I breathe, which I have never defiled with a lie.'

As the sun melts a great rock of ice on the summit of the Apennines and sends it rushing down the slope, so did the young man's impetuous anger subside at the voice of his beloved. He lowered his proud head and a torrent of tears fell from his eyes. His mother, unable to speak, held him in her arms and mingled her own tears with his. Madame de la Tour was beside herself. 'I can bear it no longer,' she said to me, 'my soul is rent in two. This ill-fated voyage must not take place. Good neighbour, will you try to take my son away. None of us here have been able to sleep for a week.'

'My friend,' I said to Paul, 'your sister will remain with us. We will speak to the governor about it tomorrow. Come and spend the night with me and let your family rest. It is late; it must be midnight for the Southern Cross is vertical to the horizon.' He let himself be led away without a word, and after a night of troubled sleep he arose with the first light and returned home.

But why should I relate any more of this story? There is never more than one side of human life that we can contemplate with pleasure. Like the globe on which we revolve, our fleeting course is no more than a day, and one part of that day can receive light only if the other is thrown into darkness.

'Father,' said I, 'I beseech you to finish telling me what you have
so affectingly begun. Images of happiness may please us but those
of misfortune instruct us. If you will, what became of this unfortunate young man?'

When Paul reached the settlement (he went on), the first object
that met his view was the Negress Marie who had climbed onto a
rock and was looking towards the open sea. As soon as he caught
sight of her, he shouted from a distance: 'Where is Virginia?'
Marie turned her head towards her young master and began to
cry. Beside himself with apprehension, Paul turned round and ran
to the harbour. There he learned that Virginia had embarked at
dawn and that her vessel had immediately set sail and could no
longer be seen. He returned to the settlement and crossed it without
a word to anyone.

Although the high rocks which enclose this valley seem to be
nearly perpendicular behind us, those green plateaux that cut
across at intervals are in fact so many steps by means of which,
following a few arduous paths, you can reach the foot of that un-
scalable cone of rocks that leans at an angle and is called Le Pouce.
At its base there is a terrace covered with tall trees, which is so high
and steep that it appears like a great forest in the air, surrounded
by dreadful precipices. The clouds that gather continually round
the summit of Le Pouce feed several streams which drop such a
way to the floor of the valley on the other side of this mountain
that from that height no sound of their fall can be heard. From this
place you can see a good part of the island and its mountains with
their rocky peaks, among them Pieter Both and the Three Paps
rising from their wooded valleys, then the open sea and the Ile
Bourbon lying forty leagues to the west. It was from this vantage-
point that Paul spied the ship that was taking Virginia away. More
than ten leagues from shore, it appeared like a black speck on the
ocean. For part of the day he remained absorbed in gazing after it,
thinking he could still see it when it had already disappeared; and
when at last it was swallowed up in the mist on the horizon, he sat
down in that desolate spot which is buffeted unceasingly by the
winds that shake the tops of the palmettos and the tacamahacs.

Their low, dull moaning, like the sound of a distant organ, inspires a deep melancholy.

There I found him (for I had been following his movements since sunrise), his head resting against the rock and his eyes fixed on the ground. It was with the greatest difficulty that I persuaded him to come down, and to return to his family. I brought him back to the settlement, where his first reaction on seeing Madame de la Tour was to complain bitterly that she had deceived him. She told us that, the wind having risen towards three o'clock in the morning and the ship being ready to get under way, the governor, accompanied by some members of his staff and the missionary, had come for Virginia in a palanquin; and that despite the protests she had made and the tears that she and Marguerite had shed, they had carried off her daughter almost expiring, amidst loud proclamations that it was for the good of the whole family.

'If at least I had been able to bid her farewell,' replied Paul, 'my mind would now be at ease. I would have said: "Virginia, if during all the time we have lived together any word has escaped my lips that has offended you, tell me, before you leave me forever, that you forgive me for it." I would have said: "Since I am fated never to see you again, farewell, my dear one, farewell. Live far from me, happy and contented." ' Then, seeing that his mother and Madame de la Tour were weeping: 'I will no longer wipe your tears,' he said, 'you must find another now;' and, with a groan, he ran away and began to roam over the settlement, visiting all the places that had been most dear to Virginia. Her goats and their kids followed him bleating. 'What is it you want?' he said. 'She who used to feed you from her hand is gone. You will never see her with me again.' When he saw the birds that fluttered about 'Virginia's Rest', he cried: 'Poor birds, no more will you fly to meet the one who cared for you so tenderly.' Watching Fidele trot before him sniffing here and there after a scent, he sighed and said: 'Never again will you find her.' Finally he went to sit on the rock where he had talked with her the night before and, at sight of the sea where he had watched her ship disappear, he broke into a torrent of weeping.

All this time we were following close behind him, fearing that the agitation of his mind might lead to some dire action. Both his mother and Virginia's implored him in the most tender terms not to add to their grief by his despair. At last Madame de la Tour managed to quieten him with a profusion of those names which were most likely to reawaken his hopes. She called him her son, her dear son, her son-in-law, her daughter's intended, urging him to come into the house and take a little nourishment. He sat down with us at the table next to the place where the companion of his childhood used to sit and, as if she were still there, he spoke to her and offered her the dishes that he knew were most to her liking; but each time he realized his mistake, he burst into tears. For some days after he gathered together everything she had kept for her personal use – the last posies she had carried, a coconut-shell cup from which she used to drink – and as if these traces of his friend had been the most precious things in the world, he would kiss them and carry them next to his bosom. The rarest perfume has not so sweet an odour as the objects touched by the object of one's love. At last, seeing that his own grief only increased that of his mother and Madame de la Tour, and that the family's needs required continual labour, he began, with Domingue's help, to repair the damage done to the garden.

Before long this young man, hitherto indifferent as a Creole to what was happening in the world, asked me to teach him to read and write so that he could correspond with Virginia. Then he wanted to acquaint himself with geography, in order to have some idea of the country where she would land, and with history, to know the manners of the people among whom she was to live. Love was his motive in these studies, as it had been when he developed his skills in agriculture and the art of laying out the most irregular piece of ground so as to make it a source of pleasure. There is no doubt that we owe most of our arts and sciences to the delights that are promised by this ardent and restless passion; and that from its disappointments was born philosophy, which teaches us how to console ourselves for every misfortune. Thus Nature, having linked all beings by love, has made it the first mover of our societies and our incitement both to knowledge and to pleasure.

Paul found that he had little taste for the study of geography

which, instead of describing the nature of each country, merely
sets forth their political divisions. He was hardly more interested
in history, least of all modern history, in which he saw only general
and recurring calamities without apparent cause, wars without
motive or object, obscure intrigues, nations without principles and
princes without humanity. He preferred the reading of novels, for
in their greater concern with human interests and feelings he sometimes discovered situations that resembled his own. Thus it was
Telemachus that pleased him more than any other book for its
portraits of rural life and the natural passions of the human heart.
In reading aloud to his mother and Madame de la Tour the
passages that affected him most he found that his own tender
memories were reawakened; then his voice would become choked
and tears would fall from his eyes. Virginia seemed to him to unite
the dignity and wisdom of Antiope with the misfortunes and the
tenderness of Eucharis. He was thrown into confusion, however, by
our fashionable novels; and when he learned that these books, full
of licentious behaviour and maxims, contained a faithful picture
of society in the countries of Europe, he began to fear, and not
without some semblance of reason, that Virginia would be corrupted there and forget him.

Indeed more than a year and a half went by before Madame
de la Tour received any news of her aunt or Virginia; she had
only learned in an indirect way that her daughter had arrived
safely in France. At last a vessel bound for the Indies brought a
parcel together with a letter written in Virginia's own hand, from
which, despite the circumspection of the amiable and generous
girl, Madame de la Tour judged her to be very unhappy. The
letter portrayed her situation and her character so well that it has
remained in my memory almost word for word :

Beloved and Dearest Mamma,
I have already written you several letters in my own hand-
writing, which I fear have never reached you as I have had no
reply. But the precautions I have now taken to send you news
of myself and to receive yours give me better hopes for this one.
Since our separation I have shed many tears, I who hardly

ever wept but for the misfortunes of others. On my arrival my great-aunt was much surprised when, having enquired about my attainments, I told her that I could neither read nor write. What then had I learned since coming into the world? she asked; and when I replied that it was to care for a household and to do your will, she said that I had been brought up like a serving-girl. The very next day she placed me as a boarder in a large abbey near Paris, where I have masters of every sort. They instruct me in history, geography, grammar, mathematics and horsemanship, among other things, but I have so little aptitude for all these subjects that I shall not profit much from the efforts of these gentlemen. I gather from their manner that they think me, what I feel I must be, a poor creature of little ability. My aunt's favours, however, have not slackened. She gives me new dresses for each season and has provided me with two chamber-maids who are as finely attired as great ladies. She has made me take the title of countess and give up the name of La Tour, which was as dear to me as it is to you, on account of all you told me of the sufferings my father had to endure in order to marry you. She has replaced it with your family name, which is also dear to me, however, because it was your name as a girl. Seeing myself in such a magnificent position, I begged my aunt to send something to relieve your need. If you had not enjoined me always to tell you the truth I could never bring myself to repeat what she said in reply. She told me that a little would be of no use to you and that, in the simple life that you lead, a lot would only be an encumbrance.

I meant at first to send you some word by another hand than mine; but as there was no one I could confide in on my arrival here, I applied myself night and day to learn to read and write and God gave me the grace to succeed in a short time. I entrusted my first letters to the ladies who attend me with instructions to dispatch them, but I have reason to believe that they were delivered to my great-aunt. This time I have the help of a friend who is also a boarder here; please send your replies to her address which is enclosed. My great-aunt has forbidden me all correspondence with the outside, saying that this could put obstacles in the way of the great plans she has for me. Apart from her, the only person who is allowed to talk to me through the grille is one of her friends, an old nobleman who, she says, is much taken with my person. But to speak truly, even if I could have a liking for someone, I have none at all for him.

I live amidst the ostentation of wealth and have not a penny of my own. I am told that it could be awkward if I had money. The very dresses I wear belong to my chambermaids, who argue over them before I have even taken them off. In the very lap of fortune I am poorer than I ever was with you, for I have nothing to give. When I saw that the fine accomplishments I was being instructed in did not bring me the means to do the slightest good, I turned to my needle which fortunately you taught me to use. I have sewed several pairs of stockings for you and for my mamma Marguerite, and I am sending them together with a cap for Domingue and one of my red handkerchiefs for Marie. I have placed in the parcel some stones and pips from the fruit we are given at supper as well as seeds from all sorts of trees which I have collected in the park of the abbey during my hours of recreation. I have added the seeds of violets, daisies, buttercups, red poppies, cornflowers and scabiouses, which I gathered in the fields. In the meadows of this country the flowers are lovelier than in ours, but no one pays the slightest attention to them. I am sure that you and my mamma Marguerite will be more pleased with this bag of seeds than with the bag of piastres which was the cause of our separation and of my tears. It will bring me great happiness if one day you have the satisfaction of seeing apple-trees growing next to our banana-trees and beeches mingling their leaves with the palms of our coconut-trees. You will think yourself in the Normandy that you love so much.

You bade me send you word of my joys and my sorrows. I have no joys far from you. As for my sorrows, I ease them by reflecting that you have placed me in my present station in obedience to God's will. But the greatest pain I have to endure is that no one here speaks to me of you and that I can speak of you to no one. My chambermaids, or rather my great-aunt's (for they are more hers than mine), say, when I try to turn the conversation to the objects that are so dear to me : 'Please remember, Mademoiselle, that you are French and that you must now forget that country of savages.' Oh! I should rather forget myself than forget the place where I was born and where you live. This country is for me a country of savages; for I live alone here, having no one to whom I can impart, dearest and beloved Mamma, the love for you that will be borne to the grave by

Your obedient and affectionate daughter,
Virginia de la Tour

I commend to your kind attention Marie and Domingue who cared so well for me in childhood. Caress Fidele who found me in the woods.

Paul was greatly surprised that Virginia had made no mention at all of him, when she had kept a place in her remembrances for the house-dog. He did not know that, however long a woman's letter, she always reserves her most cherished thought for the end.

In a postscript Virginia particularly recommended to Paul two kinds of seeds, those of the violet and the scabious; she explained their characteristics and gave him instructions on the most favourable places to sow them. 'The violet,' she wrote, 'produces a small flower of a deep violet colour which likes to conceal itself under bushes but is soon discovered by its enchanting perfume.' She wished him expressly to sow it beside the pool, at the foot of her coconut-tree. 'The scabious,' she added, 'produces pretty pale-blue flowers which stand out against a black background dotted with white. It seems to be in mourning and for that reason is also known as the widow's flower. It thrives in rough, wind-swept places.' She asked him to sow it on the rock where she had spoken to him for the last time the night before her departure and to name the spot 'Farewell Rock', for love of her.

She had enclosed the seeds in a little purse made of the simplest cloth, but which seemed priceless to Paul when he noticed on it a P and a V interlaced and fashioned of hair which he recognized by its beauty to be Virginia's own.

All the family shed tears over the letter of this virtuous and tender-hearted young lady. Her mother replied, on behalf of them all, that she should remain or return as she wished, assuring her that her departure had deprived them of the best part of their happiness, and that she especially was inconsolable.

Paul wrote a very long letter to Virginia in which he promised to improve the garden so as to make it worthy of her, mingling the plants of Europe with those of Africa just as she had interlaced their initials in her needlework. From the coconut-trees that grew beside her pool, he sent her some of the fruit which had developed to a perfect ripeness, adding that he had included no other seeds from the island so that the desire to see the plants they produced might prompt her to an early return. He entreated her to comply as soon as possible with the ardent wishes of their family, and with his own, as he would never experience happiness again away from her.

Paul planted the European seeds with the greatest care, especially those of the violet and the scabious whose flowers seemed to bear some resemblance to the character and the present situation of Virginia, who had recommended them so particularly to him. But, whether they had been spoiled by exposure during the voyage or, what is more likely, the climate of this part of Africa was unfavourable to them, only a small number germinated and even these never reached their full growth.

Meanwhile envy, which seems to seek out human happiness, especially in the French colonies, spread rumours over the island which worried Paul greatly. The officers and crew of the vessel that had brought Virginia's letter gave it out that she was about to marry, even naming the nobleman of the court who was to make her his wife; some went so far as to say that the thing was already done and that they had witnessed it themselves. At first Paul scorned this news, brought as it was by a trading ship, which so often spreads falsehoods in the places it touches on its passage; but as several of the settlers, from a kind of pity that was not unmixed with treachery, showed themselves eager to condole with him over the event, he began to have some belief in it himself. Moreover, he had seen that infidelity was treated as a jest in some of the novels

he had read; and as he knew that by and large these books portrayed European manners accurately, he feared that Madame de
la Tour's daughter would be corrupted there and forget her former
engagements. Already the knowledge he had acquired was making
him unhappy. What brought his growing fears to their highest
point, however, was that several ships from Europe arrived in the
six months following without bringing any news of Virginia.

An unhappy prey to every agitation of his heart, the young man
would often come to see me, seeking to confirm or to dispel his
misgivings by my experience of the world.

I live, as I have already told you, one and a half leagues from here
on the banks of a little river that runs along the foot of the Long
Mountain. There I pass my days alone, without wife, children,
or slaves.

If we except the rare good fortune of finding a partner who is
well suited to us, surely the least unhappy state of life is to live
alone. Every man who has had much to complain of in his dealings
with men seeks out solitude; and it is remarkable that all those
peoples who have been made unhappy by their opinions, their
manners or their governments have produced numerous classes
of citizens entirely devoted to solitude and to celibacy. Such were
the Egyptians in their decline and the Greeks of the Later Empire,
and such in our own day are the Indians, the Chinese, the modern
Greeks, the Italians and most of the peoples of eastern and southern
Europe. Solitude restores a part of man's natural happiness by
removing him from the turmoil of social life. In the midst of our
societies, which are divided by so many prejudices, the soul is
permanently in a state of agitation, ceaselessly turning over within
itself the thousand turbulent and contradictory opinions by which
the members of an ambitious and contemptible society seek to
reduce each other to subjection. In solitude it puts off these extran-
eous and troubling illusions and regains a simple sense of itself,
of Nature and of its Maker. In like manner the muddy water of a
torrent that ravages the countryside, when it happens to fill some
small hollow apart from its usual course, deposits its silt on the

bottom of its basin, recovers its original clarity and, become transparent once again, reflects, together with its own banks, the greenery of the earth and the light of the heavens.

Solitude restores the harmonies of the body as well as those of
the soul. Among the class of men who live in seclusion are to be
found those who, like the brahmins of India, have enjoyed the
longest span of life. So necessary do I consider it to happiness, even
in the world itself, that it seems to me impossible to experience a
lasting pleasure of any kind whatever or to regulate our conduct
on any fixed principle unless we create for ourselves an inner solitude, allowing our opinions to issue from it only very rarely and
forbidding entry entirely to those of others. I do not mean to say
that man should live in complete isolation. His needs link him to
the rest of humankind and he therefore owes his work to other
men. He has also a duty to the rest of nature. But as God has given
to each of us organs that are perfectly suited to the elements of the
globe on which we live – feet for the ground, lungs for the air,
eyes for the light, and whose functions we are powerless to change –
so has He reserved for Himself alone, as the Author of life, the
heart, which is its principal organ.

And so I pass my days far from men, whom I wished to serve,
and who persecuted me. After I had travelled through a good part
of Europe and some regions of America and Africa, I settled on
this sparsely-populated island, enchanted by its mild climate and
its solitary places. A cabin that I built in the forest at the foot of a
tree, a small field cleared with my own hands and a river that
flows past my door, suffice for my needs and my pleasures. To
these I add the enjoyment of a few good books, which not only
teach me to become better but make the very world I have left
behind promote my happiness; for by keeping before my mind
images of the passions that cause the wretchedness of its citizens,
they allow me to enjoy a negative happiness when I compare their
lot with mine. Like a shipwrecked man who has climbed to safety
on a rock, I contemplate from my solitude the storms that rage
through the rest of the world, and my tranquillity redoubles at the
distant sound of the tempest. Now that men no longer stand in my
way, nor I in theirs, I have stopped hating them; I pity them

instead. If I chance to meet someone in adversity, I try to help him by my advice, just as a man passing along the bank of a rushing stream stretches forth his hand to an unlucky creature who is drowning in it. But I have found that my voice is hardly ever heeded, except by innocence. Nature calls in vain to the majority of men; each one fashions for himself an image of her which he clothes in his own passions. All his life he pursues this empty shadow which leads him astray, and then complains to Heaven for the error he has himself created. Among the great number of unfortunate men whom I have from time to time attempted to lead back to Nature, I have not found a single one who was not intoxicated with his own misery. At first they listened to me with attention in the hope that I might help them to acquire glory or fortune, but when they understood that these were the very things I wanted to teach them to do without, they supposed me a poor wretch myself for not running after their sorry happiness. They found fault with my solitary life; they claimed that they alone were useful to mankind and did their best to draw me into the whirlwind with them. But if I share my thoughts with everyone, I surrender my independence to no one. Often I need look no further than myself to find all the lessons that I need. In my present tranquillity I bring before my mind the agitations of my own past life, which once I prized so highly: patronage, fortune, reputation, luxury and the opinions that clash in every part of the world. I compare the numbers of men that I have watched struggling furiously with each other for these chimeras, and who are no more, to the waves that break into foam against the rocks in my river and disappear, never to return. I prefer to let myself be carried along in peace by the current of time towards the shoreless ocean of the future and, by contemplating the present harmonies of Nature, to rise towards the Author of them, hoping for a happier destiny in another world.

From my solitary dwelling in the midst of a forest I cannot see the multitude of objects which this high place presents to the view; yet the surroundings are not without interest, especially for a man like me who prefers to retire into himself rather than go much into the world. The river that flows past my door continues in a straight line through the woods, looking like a long canal shaded by trees with every sort of foliage : there are tacamahacs, ebony-trees and those that we call apple-wood, olive-wood and cinnamon-wood. Here and there the bare columns of a grove of palmettos rise more than a hundred feet to the clusters of palms at their tops and appear above the surrounding trees like another forest planted on the one below. Creepers of various kinds intertwine between the trees, forming in one place arcades of blossoms and in another long curtains of greenery. Most of the trees give off aromatic odours which penetrate even the clothes one wears, so that you can tell a man has passed through a forest several hours after he has left it. In the season when the trees are in flower you would think them half covered with snow. At the end of summer several species of foreign birds arrive, guided from some unknown regions beyond the vast seas by a mysterious instinct, to feed on the seeds of the island's vegetation, their brilliant colours thrown into relief by the sun-darkened foliage of the trees. Among others, there are various species of parakeets and the blue pigeons that are known here as Dutch pigeons. The monkeys who have settled in these forests romp in the dark branches, where they stand out with their grey and greenish coats and their pure black faces. Some swing by their tails from the limbs of trees whilst others leap from branch to branch carrying their young in their arms. The murderous gun has never frightened these peaceful children of Nature. Here nothing can be heard but cries of joy and the unfamiliar warbling and cooing of a few birds from southern lands, which are repeated from a distance by the echoes of the forest. The river runs foaming over its bed of rock, passing through the trees and reflecting here and there in its limpid waters their venerable masses of greenery and of shade as well as the happy play of the creatures that dwell in them. A thousand paces farther on it rushes over a series of rock shelves, forming as it falls a sheet of water flawless as crystal which bursts into bubbles of foam as it strikes the pool below. A thousand mingled sounds rise from these tumultuous waters and are carried by the winds into the forest where sometimes they fade into the distance and sometimes crowd all at once upon the ear in a deafening chorus like the sound of cathedral bells. The air, which is continually freshened by the movement of the waters, maintains on the banks of this river, despite the burning heat of summer, a greenery and coolness rarely found on the island, even on the tops of the mountains.

Not far away there stands a rock, which is distant enough from the cascade so that one is not deafened by the roar yet near enough to have a view of it and to enjoy the coolness and the murmuring of the waters. When summer was at its hottest, Madame de la Tour, Marguerite, Virginia, Paul and myself would sometimes take our midday meal in the shade of this rock. Virginia, who performed her most ordinary actions with the good of others in mind, would never eat fruit in the country without burying the stones or the pips in the earth. 'They will produce trees,' she would say, 'which will give their fruit to some traveller, or at least to a bird.' One day when she had eaten a papaw, she planted its seeds at the foot of this rock. Not long afterwards, several papaw-trees sprang up, among them a female, which is the one that bears fruit. At Virginia's departure this tree hardly came up to her knee, but it grows rapidly and two years later had reached a height of twenty feet with several rings of ripe fruit round the upper part of its trunk. Having gone to this place by chance, Paul was filled with joy when he beheld the tall tree which had grown from the small seed he had seen planted by his friend; at the same time a profound sadness came over him at this evidence of her long absence. It is not the objects that we see habitually which make us conscious of the rapidity of our lives; they grow old with us by imperceptible degrees; but those that we suddenly see again after the lapse of a few years give us warning of the speed with which the river of our days is flowing away. Paul was as surprised and troubled to see the tall papaw-tree laden with fruit as a traveller who returns to his country after a long absence to find not the friends of his youth but their children, who were babes at the breast when he went away, now fathers of families themselves. Sometimes he wanted to cut it down, for it was too painful a reminder of the length of time that had passed since Virginia's departure; at other times, regarding it as a monument to her active goodness, he would kiss the trunk and address it with words of love and regret.

O tree, whose posterity still stands in our woods, I have looked upon you myself with more tender interest and veneration than the triumphal arches of the Romans! May Nature, which every day destroys the monuments of kingly ambition, increase in our forests those of a poor girl's kind actions!

It was at the foot of this papaw-tree that I was sure to meet Paul whenever he came into my neighbourhood. One day, finding him there gloomy and dejected, I had a conversation with him which I should like to recount to you, if you don't find these long digressions of mine too tedious. But perhaps an old man may be pardoned for remembering his last friendships. I shall relate it in the form of a dialogue so that you may appreciate the young man's natural good sense. You will easily distinguish the speakers by the gist of his questions and my replies. He said to me:

'Mademoiselle de la Tour's absence is like a great weight on my heart. It is now two years and two months since she went away and eight and a half months since we had any word from her. I am poor, she is rich and has forgotten me. How I long to board a ship that will take me to France! Once there, I can make my fortune by serving the king, and when I have become a great nobleman, Mademoiselle de la Tour's great-aunt will give her to me in marriage.'

THE OLD MAN

'My friend, did you not tell me that you were of humble birth?'

PAUL

'So my mother told me; but I am not at all clear in my own mind about this question of birth. I have never noticed that I was of lower birth than anyone else, or that others were of higher birth than me.'

THE OLD MAN

'In France obscure birth would bar your way to high office; what

is more, you could not even be admitted to any of the distinguished
Corps of the state.'

PAUL

'But you have told me many times that one of the causes of France's
greatness was that there were no limits to what the very least of
the king's subjects might achieve; you even cited the names of
many famous men who had risen from modest beginnings to bring
honour to their country. Were you misleading me, then, by this en-
couragement?'

THE OLD MAN

'My son, I shall never seek to dishearten you. What I said was true
about former times, but now things have changed greatly. Nowadays in France everything has a price on it and whatever is not
the inherited privilege of a few families is allotted to the Corps.
The king is a sun, but the great nobles and the Corps are like
clouds gathered round him, making it nearly impossible for one of
his rays to shine on you. In the past the administration was less
complicated and the things that I described to you were not un-
heard of. Then talent and merit flourished on all sides, just as new
land which has been freshly cleared for cultivation yields with all its
vigour. But great kings, those who understand men and how to
choose them, are rare; the common sort can be moved only by the
influence of the nobles or the Corps that surround them.'

PAUL

'Perhaps I can find one of these great men who will be my protector?'

THE OLD MAN

'To gain the protection of the great you must either further their
ambition or satisfy their pleasures; but your humble birth will
always prevent you from succeeding in the one and your integrity
in the other.'

PAUL

'But I shall perform actions so courageous, I shall be so true to my word, so exact in my duties, so devoted and so constant in my friendship, that one of them will recognize my worth and adopt me. I saw that this was the practice in the books of ancient history that you gave me to read.'

THE OLD MAN

'Ah, my friend, among the Greeks and Romans, even in their decadence, virtue was respected by the great; but although we have had a host of famous men of every kind from among the common people, I do not know of a single one who had been adopted by a great family. Without the patronage of our kings, virtue in France would be condemned to remain forever plebeian. As I told you, they honour it sometimes, when it comes to their notice, but nowadays the distinctions that were once accorded to virtue are only to be had for money.'

PAUL

'If no great man will help me, I will try to gain favour with one of the Corps. I will win its affection by wholly adopting its spirit and its opinions.'

THE OLD MAN

'You will do what other men have done, betray your conscience to make your way in the world?'

PAUL

'Oh, no! I will never seek anything but the truth.'

THE OLD MAN

'Then you may well find that hatred rather than love is your reward. The Corps are very little concerned with the discovery of truth. All opinions are alike to ambitious men, provided they can govern.'

PAUL

'This is misfortune indeed! I am rebuffed everywhere and condemned to pass my days in obscure labour, far from Virginia.' (Here he fetched a deep sigh.)

THE OLD MAN

'Let God be your only patron and humankind your Corps. Be constant in your attachment to one and the other. Families, Corps, nations, kings – all have their prejudices and their passions; to serve them one must often be guilty of vice. God and humankind ask only virtue of us.

'But why do you want to distinguish yourself from the rest of men? Such a feeling is not natural, for if it were shared by all, every man would be at war with his neighbour. Be content to do your duty in the station where Providence has placed you and be thankful for a life in which your conscience is your own. Your happiness does not depend, like that of the rich, on the opinion of those beneath you; nor are you obliged, like the poor, to grovel before the great for your means of subsistence. In this country and in your circumstances you have enough to live on without deceiving or flattering, or demeaning yourself, as most of those must do who seek fortune in Europe. Your condition is compatible with every virtue. You need have no fear of being good, true, sincere, learned, patient, temperate, chaste, lenient, pious; no ridicule will come to blight your discretion, which is just beginning to flower. Heaven has given you freedom, health, a clear conscience and friends; the kings whose favour you long to win are not so fortunate as you are.'

PAUL

'Ah, but from all this Virginia is missing. Without her I have nothing; with her I should have everything. She alone is high birth, glory and fortune to me. But since her aunt wants to marry her to a man with a great name, I will apply myself to the study of books, for with their help one can become learned and distinguished. I will acquire knowledge, I will render useful service to my country by what I have learned, harming no one and depending on no one; and when I have become famous my glory will belong to me alone.'

THE OLD MAN

'Talents, my son, are rarer even than high birth and riches and are certainly a greater good, for nothing can take them from us and everywhere they meet with public esteem. But they exact a high price. To develop them we must endure every sort of privation and have an exquisite sensibility which renders us both inwardly unhappy and an object of persecution for our contemporaries. In France the lawyer does not covet the glory of the soldier, nor the soldier the glory of the seaman, but when you are there everyone will put obstacles in your path because there everyone prides himself on his intellect and understanding. You want to serve your fellow-men, you say? But he who makes a field produce one more sheaf of corn renders them a greater service than he who gives them a book.'

PAUL

'Oh, she who planted this papaw-tree gave to those who dwell in these forests a gift that is sweeter and more useful than a whole library of books.' (As he spoke these words, he threw his arms round the tree and kissed it rapturously.)

THE OLD MAN

'The best of books, the Gospel, which preaches only equality, friendship, humanity and peace, has for centuries served as a pretext for the wrath of Europeans. Only think how much public and private tyranny is still carried on in its name in every part of the earth! After that, who will flatter himself that his book may be beneficial to men? Remember the fate of most of the philosophers who preached wisdom to mankind. Homer, who clothed it in such beautiful verses, was reduced to begging. Socrates, whose discourse and conduct gave so many gentle lessons to the Athenians, was by them sentenced to death by poisoning, and his sublime disciple Plato was delivered into slavery by order of the very prince who protected him. Before them, Pythagoras, whose idea of humanity extended to the beasts themselves, was burnt alive by the Crotonians. And this is not all : the greater part even of these illustrious names have come down to us with their characters disfigured by strokes of satire, and human ingratitude is pleased to find them so. If the glory of a few names out of so many has been passed on to us pure and unspotted, it is because those who bore them lived far from the society of their contemporaries, like those statues which are recovered whole from the fields of Greece and Italy and which have escaped the barbarians' fury by being buried in the bosom of the earth.

'So you see that to achieve the turbulent glory of literature great virtue is needed, as well as readiness to lay down one's life. Moreover, you must not think that in France the rich take any interest in this glory. What do they care for men of letters whose knowledge brings them, in their own country, no dignity or position of authority or admission to court? If in this century indifferent to everything but riches and pleasure, there is little persecution, neither is there any distinction to be gained by learning and virtue in a country where money buys everything. In former times they were sure to find their reward in the various offices of the Church, the judiciary or the administration; nowadays they are useful for nothing else but the writing of books. And yet these fruits of so much labour, however little prized by the world, are nonetheless worthy of their celestial origins. For books have as their proper function to give lustre to obscure virtue, to console the unfortunate, to enlighten nations and to speak the truth even to kings. This is without question the noblest calling with which Heaven can honour a mortal on earth. Is there an author who has not found consolation for the injustice or the contempt of those who possess great wealth in the thought that from century to century and from nation to nation his work will serve as a bulwark against error and tyranny, and that from the midst of the obscurity in which he has lived will shine forth a glory that will eclipse that of most kings, whose monuments perish in oblivion in spite of the flatterers who raise and extol them?'

PAUL

'Oh, I would seek glory only to shower it on Virginia and make her dear to all the world. But you who know so much, tell me whether we shall ever be married. I should like to be a learned man, if only to know the future.'

THE OLD MAN

'My son, who would want to live if he knew the future? The expectation of a single misfortune causes us so much unnecessary anxiety that the prospect of certain calamity would poison every day that preceded it. We must not enquire too deeply, even into the world about us. Heaven, which gave us the intelligence to foresee our needs, has given us those needs to set limits to our intelligence.'

PAUL

'You say that with money one can acquire dignities and honours in Europe. If I cross to Bengal and make a fortune there, I can then go to Paris and marry Virginia. I must embark without delay.'

THE OLD MAN

'What! and leave her mother and yours?'

PAUL

'But you advised me yourself to go to the Indies.'

THE OLD MAN

'At that time Virginia was still here. Now your mother and hers are entirely dependent on you.'

PAUL

'Virginia's rich relation will provide her with the means to help them.'

THE OLD MAN

'The rich help very few but those who honour them in the eyes of the world. They have relations who are far more to be pitied than Madame de la Tour and who are obliged, for want of assistance, to sacrifice their freedom for bread and spend their lives shut up in convents.'

PAUL

'What a place is this Europe! Oh, Virginia must return home! What need has she of a rich relation? She was so happy in our cabins, so pretty and so perfectly attired with a red handkerchief or a few flowers round her head. Come back, Virginia! Leave magnificence and great houses behind you and return to these rocks, to the shade of these woods and of our coconut-trees. Alas! Perhaps you are unhappy at this very moment . . .' (and he began to weep). 'Father, keep nothing from me; if you cannot say whether I shall marry Virginia, at least tell me whether she can still love me when she is surrounded by great noblemen who converse with the king and who come to visit her?'

THE OLD MAN

'Ah! my friend, I am sure that she loves you for many reasons, but above all because she is virtuous.' (At these words he fell on my neck, transported with delight.)

PAUL

'But do you think that European women are false, as they are made out to be in the comedies and books that you lent me?'

THE OLD MAN

'Women are false in those countries where men are tyrants. Force, wherever it is exercised, produces deceit.'

PAUL

'How can men be tyrants to women?'

THE OLD MAN

'By marrying them without their consent, a young girl to an old man, a woman of feeling to a man without a heart.'

PAUL

'Why not marry those who are suited to each other? the young with the young, lover with lover?'

THE OLD MAN

'Because most young people in France are without sufficient fortune to marry and by the time they have acquired enough they have grown old. As young men they corrupt their neighbours' wives; when they are old they cannot secure their own wives' affection. Having deceived others in youth, they are themselves deceived in old age. This reaction is part of the universal justice that governs the world where excess is always counterbalanced by excess. Most Europeans pass their lives in this twofold state of moral disorder; and it is a state that increases in proportion as the riches of a society are concentrated in the hands of a few individuals. A nation is like a garden in which small trees cannot grow if there are too many tall ones to overshadow them: with this difference, that a small number of tall trees can create the beauty of a garden, whereas the prosperity of a nation will always depend upon the equality of a great number of subjects and not upon the riches of a few.'

PAUL

'But why must they wait until they are rich before they marry?'

THE OLD MAN

'So that they can pass their days in plenty and idleness.'

PAUL

'Why do they not work? I certainly do.'

THE OLD MAN

'Because in Europe manual labour – or mechanical labour as it is called – is considered dishonourable; and the most despised of all work is the tilling of the earth. An artisan is held in much higher regard there than a peasant.'

PAUL

'What! the art that feeds men is despised in Europe! How can this be? I don't understand.'

THE OLD MAN

'It is impossible for a man raised in a state of nature to understand how society can deprave. He forms an exact conception of order but not of disorder. Beauty, virtue and happiness have form and shape for him; ugliness, vice and unhappiness have none.'

PAUL

'Then how happy the rich must be! They encounter no obstacles; they can fill the lives of those they love with pleasures.'

THE OLD MAN

'In most of them the appetite for every pleasure has been blunted by the very fact that they cost them no trouble. Have you not found

that the pleasure of rest must be bought with fatigue, the pleasure
of eating with hunger, that of drinking with thirst? Well, that of
loving and of being loved can only be procured by a multitude of
privations and sacrifices. The rich are cut off from these pleasures
by their wealth which anticipates their every need. To the weariness that follows satiety they join the pride that is born of opulence
and which the slightest privation wounds, even after its appetite
for the greatest pleasures has been blunted. The scent of a
thousand roses pleases only for an instant, but the pain caused by a
single one of their thorns continues long after one has been pricked.
A pain amidst their pleasures is for the rich a thorn among flowers,
whilst for the poor a pleasure amidst their pains is a flower among
thorns, and they savour it with the keenest enjoyment. Every effect
is increased by its opposite. Nature has balanced all things. When
all is taken into account, which state seems to you preferable – to
have practically nothing to hope for and everything to fear, or
practically nothing to fear and everything to hope for? The first
state is that of the rich, the second that of the poor. But these
extremes are equally hard for human beings to bear; happiness is to
be found in the mean between them and in the practice of virtue.'

PAUL

'What do you mean by virtue?'

THE OLD MAN

'My son, you who support your family by your labours have no
need of a definition. Virtue is an effort of the will which we make
for the good of others with the intention of pleasing God alone.'

PAUL

'How virtuous is Virginia, then! It was virtue that made her want
to become rich so that she could do good to others. It was virtue
that made her leave this island, and virtue will bring her back.'

The idea that Virginia would return before long took hold of
the young man's imagination and one by one his misgivings began

to vanish : the reason she had not written was that she had already started for home, and with a good wind the journey from Europe took no time at all. He would recite the names of the vessels that had completed the passage of four thousand five hundred leagues in less than three months. Of course the ship on which she was travelling would require no more than two : the shipbuilders nowadays were so expert and the sailors so skilful. He talked of the arrangements he would make to welcome her, of the new cabin he was going to build, of the pleasures and surprises he would prepare every day for her when she was his wife. His wife! he was ravished by the idea. 'At all events, Father,' he would say, 'you will no longer need to do anything but what pleases you. With Virginia's riches we shall have plenty of blacks who will work for you. You will remain with us always and have no other care but to amuse and enjoy yourself.' And, in a state of exaltation, he would go to share his delirious joy with his family.

Great hopes soon give way to great fears and violent passions always throw the soul into the opposite extreme. Often Paul would call on me again the following day, sad and dejected. 'I have had no word from Virginia,' he would say. 'If she had left Europe, she would have written to let me know. Ah! the rumours that circulated about her were only too well founded. Her aunt has married her to a great nobleman. Love of riches has ruined her like so many others. In those books of yours which portray women so well, virtue is no more than a romantic fiction. If Virginia had been virtuous she would never have left her mother and me. While I spend my life thinking of her, she has forgotten me. I am wretched, and she enjoys herself. Oh! the thought of it brings me to despair. I have lost all taste for work; the company of others wearies me. Please God that war is declared in India. I would go there and die.'

'My son,' I replied, 'the courage that makes us throw ourselves into the jaws of death is no more than the courage of a moment. It is often prompted by the vain applause of men. But there is another and rarer kind of courage which is more necessary because it helps us to bear the reverses of life each day without witnesses and without praise : this is patience. It is founded neither on the opinions of others nor on the impulse of our passions but on the will of God. Patience is the courage of virtue.'

'Oh, then I have no virtue,' he cried, 'for I am cast down and disheartened by everything.'

'It is not man's lot', I went on, 'to possess virtue, which is always impartial, constant and unchanging. Under the influence of the many passions that shake us our reason clouds and darkens, but there are beacons at which its torch can be lighted again : the great works of literature.

'Literature, my son, is Heaven-sent assistance. The works of the great authors are beams of the wisdom that governs the universe, which mankind, inspired by divine art, has learned to maintain on earth. Like the rays of the sun their divine fire gives light, warmth and gladness. And like fire, they adapt all nature to our use. Through them we can gather round us all times, places, men and objects. They recall to us the rules of human conduct, quieten the passions, repress vice and incite us to virtue by the noble examples of upright men and women which they celebrate in literary portraits that continue to be honoured. Literature is the daughter of Heaven, who has come down to earth to lighten the troubles of the human race. The great authors whom she inspires have always appeared in those times which all societies find most difficult to bear, times of barbarism and of depravity. Innumerable men unhappier than you are, my son, have found consolation in literature : Xenophon, exiled from his homeland after leading back ten thousand of his countrymen; Scipio Africanus, weary of the calumnies of the Romans; Lucullus of their intrigues; Catinat of the ingratitude of the court. The ingenious Greeks assigned to each of the Muses of literature the direction of a part of our understanding; we should, in like manner, allow them to govern our passions; they should yoke and bridle them, fulfilling the same function, in relation to the faculties of our souls, as the Hours who harnessed and led the horses of the sun.

'Read then, my son. The wise men who have written are travellers who have gone before us in the paths of adversity. They stretch forth their hands and invite us to join their company when all else has forsaken us. A good book is a good friend.'

'Ah!' cried Paul, 'I had no need of books when Virginia was here. She had read no more than I had, but when she looked at me and called me her friend it was impossible for my heart to be heavy.'

'To be sure,' I said, 'there is no friend so agreeable as a woman who returns our love. Moreover, there is in woman a light-hearted cheerfulness which relieves the melancholy of man. Her graces drive away the dark spectres of reflection. Her face shines with gentle charms and confidence. Is there any joy that is not made keener by her joy? any frown that does not brighten at her smile? any anger that can resist her tears? Virginia will return with more philosophy than you have. She will be greatly surprised not to find the garden in perfect order again, she who thinks only of beautifying it in spite of the persecutions of her great-aunt, which she must endure far from her mother and from you.'

The thought that Virginia would soon return revived Paul's spirits. He went back to his rustic tasks, happy, in spite of his cares, to be working towards an object that was pleasing to his heart.

One morning at first light (it was 24 December, 1744) Paul saw, on rising, that a white flag had been raised on Discovery Mountain. As this was the signal that a vessel had been sighted at sea, he ran to the town to see if it brought any news of Virginia. He remained there until evening waiting for the return of the harbour pilot who had followed the usual practice of going out to identify the ship. The pilot reported to the governor that it was the *Saint-Géran* which had been sighted, a vessel of seven hundred tons commanded by a captain named Monsieur Aubin; she was four leagues outside the harbour and would not drop anchor at Port Louis until the following afternoon, and then only if there was a favourable wind. At that moment not a breeze was stirring. The pilot delivered to the governor the letters that the ship had brought from France. One of them was addressed to Madame de la Tour in Virginia's hand. Paul seized it at once and kissed it rapturously; then, putting it next to his bosom, he ran to the settlement. The family were awaiting his return on 'Farewell Rock'. As soon as he caught sight of them Paul, unable to speak, waved the letter above his head. They all gathered in Madame de la Tour's cabin to hear it read. Virginia informed her mother that she had suffered much ill-usage at the hands of her great-aunt, who had first wanted to marry her against her will, then disinherited her and finally sent her back to the Ile de France at a time when her arrival would coincide with the hurricane season. She had tried to soften her aunt's determination by pointing out what she owed to her mother and to the habits she had learned in childhood, but all in vain; she had been declared a foolish girl whose mind had been corrupted by reading novels. She now cared for nothing but the joy of seeing and embracing her dear family once more, and she would have satisfied her ardent desire that very day if the captain had allowed her to come ashore in the pilot's launch; but he had been unwilling to do so because of the great distance to land and the heavy seas outside the harbour, despite the absence of wind.

No sooner was the letter read than all the family cried : 'Virginia has come home!' and threw their arms round each other in transports of joy, mistresses and servants together. 'My son,' said Madame de la Tour to Paul, 'go and inform our neighbour of Virginia's arrival.' At once Domingue lit a torch of round-wood and he and Paul set off for my settlement.

It must have been around ten o'clock at night. I had just extinguished my lamp and retired to bed when through the logs of my cabin wall I perceived a light in the woods. Soon after, I heard Paul's voice calling me. I rose and had hardly finished dressing when he fell on my neck, beside himself and all out of breath : 'Come along,' he said, 'Virginia has arrived. Come with me to the harbour; her ship will anchor at daybreak.'

We set off at once. As we were crossing the woods below the Long Mountain, having already joined the road that leads from Pamplemousses to the port, I heard the sound of steps behind us and turned to see a Negro advancing with long strides. As soon as he drew level with us I asked him where he was coming from and where he was going in such a hurry. 'I come from the district called La Poudre d'Or, in the north of the island,' he replied. 'I have been sent to notify the governor that a vessel from France is lying at anchor in a very bad sea leeward of the Ile d'Ambre. She is firing her cannon to signal for help.' Having told us this, the man hurried on his way.

'The Poudre d'Or district is no more than three leagues from here,' I said to Paul; 'let us go directly there and meet Virginia.'

The heat was stifling as we set off towards the north. The moon had risen, and was encircled by three great black rings. The sky was dreadfully dark. In the frequent flashes of lightning we could make out long lines of dark, thick cloud low in the sky, coming in from the sea with great speed and banking up near the middle of the island, although on the ground not the slightest breeze could be felt. As we continued on our way we heard what seemed to be the rolling of thunder but, after listening more closely, we recognized the booming of a cannon repeated by the echoes. These far-off sounds, together with the stormy aspect of the sky, made me shudder. There could be no doubt that they were the distress-signals of a vessel in danger of sinking. Half an hour later the cannon ceased firing altogether, and the silence seemed to me even more frightening than the doleful sounds that had preceded it.

We hastened on without a word, neither of us daring to impart his fears to the other, and when, around midnight, we reached the seashore in the Poudre d'Or district, we were bathed in sweat. The waves were breaking with a terrifying sound, covering the rocks and the beach with dazzling white foam and with sparks of fire by whose phosphorescent gleams we could make out, in spite of the deep gloom, the long canoes of the fishermen which had been pulled well up on the sand.

Some distance away, near the edge of the wood, we saw a fire around which several settlers had gathered. There we repaired to rest ourselves and wait for morning. While we were seated by the fire one of the settlers told us how that afternoon he had watched the currents carry a ship from the open sea towards the island. Since nightfall she could no longer be seen but two hours after sunset he had heard her firing a cannon to call for help; so rough was the sea, however, that no boat could put out to try to reach her. Soon after, he thought he had seen the light from a ship's lanterns which, he feared, could only mean that, having come so close to land, she had gone in between the shore and the little Ile d'Ambre, mistaking it for the Coin de Mire, near which vessels pass when they put in at Port Louis. If this was the case – and he could not say for certain that it was – then the ship was in the greatest peril. Another settler spoke up, saying that he had crossed the channel that separates the Ile d'Ambre from the coast several times; and that, judging from the soundings he had taken, the anchorage was very good and solid and the ship was perfectly safe there, as if she had been in the best harbour. 'I would risk my entire fortune on her,' he added, 'and sleep on board as peacefully as on dry land.' A third settler said that it was impossible for a ship to enter the channel, which even launches could scarcely navigate. He was sure that he had seen her drop anchor beyond the Ile d'Ambre, so that if the wind happened to rise in the morning she would be in a position either to put out to sea or make for the harbour. Other settlers offered other opinions, wrangling among themselves in the manner of idle Creoles, but all the while Paul and I remained perfectly silent. We stayed where we were until the first light of dawn, but the sky was not at all bright and the sea was covered with mist so that we could make out nothing on it but a dark mass a quarter of a league from the coast which, we were told, was the Ile d'Ambre. Indeed so thick was the gloom on the island itself that we could see no more than the headland where we were gathered and the peaks of a few mountains in the interior, which emerged now and again from the clouds that swirled around them.

Towards seven o'clock in the morning the sound of drums in the woods announced the approach of the governor, Monsieur de la Bourdonnais. He arrived on horseback, followed by a detachment of soldiers armed with muskets and a large number of settlers and blacks. Drawing up the soldiers on the shore, he ordered them to fire their pieces all at once. No sooner had they discharged their arms than we perceived a flash on the sea, followed almost immediately by the sound of a cannon. We reckoned that the ship could not be far from us and we all ran in the direction in which we had seen her signal until through the fog we discerned the hull and yards of a large vessel. She was so close to shore that, despite the noise of the waves, we could hear the boatswain's whistle as he gave his orders and the shouts of the sailors, who cried out three times, 'Long live the King'; this being the cry of Frenchmen in moments of extreme peril as well as of great joy, as if in times of danger they called to their prince to help them or wished to show their willingness to lay down their lives for him.

The moment the *Saint-Géran* realized that we were near enough to give assistance, she began to fire a cannon every three minutes. Monsieur de la Bourdonnais had great fires lit at intervals along the beach and sent to all the neighbouring settlements for food, planks, cables and empty casks. A crowd of settlers soon arrived from the nearby districts of Poudre d'Or, Flacque and Rampart River; they were accompanied by their slaves, who were laden with provisions and tackle. One of the settlers who had lived longest on the island approached the governor and said : 'Monsieur, all night long we have heard rumblings from the mountain; in the woods the leaves are stirring on the trees although no wind is blowing; the sea-birds are sheltering on land : these signs always mean that a hurricane is coming.' 'If it comes, my friends,' replied the governor, 'we shall be ready for it, and surely the vessel will be too.'

Indeed there was every indication that a hurricane was approaching. Directly overhead we could make out clouds that were horribly black in the centre and copper-coloured round the edges. The air rang with the cries of tropic-birds, frigates, scissor-bills and a multitude of other sea-birds who were arriving from every point of the horizon, despite the darkness of the atmosphere, to seek refuge on the island.

Towards nine o'clock in the morning we heard the most frightful noises from out at sea, as if torrents mixed with thunder had rolled down from the mountain-tops. 'Hurricane!' cried everyone at once, and an instant later a dreadful whirlwind carried away the mist that covered the Ile d'Ambre and its channel, revealing the *Saint-Géran*. Her yards and topmasts had been lowered; her deck was crowded with people, her flag at half-mast. She was held at anchor by four forward cables and a bower-cable behind, between

the Ile d'Ambre and land, within the belt of reefs that encloses the
Ile de France and through which she had passed at a point where
no vessel had ever gone before. As her bows were turned towards
the open sea, each wave that entered the channel lifted her prow
clear of the water revealing the underside of her hull; and at the
same moment her poop, plunging into the water, disappeared from
view right up to the taffrail, as if submerged. Her position was
impossible : being forced towards the shore by the wind and the
sea, she could neither go out the way she had come in nor cut her
lines and run aground on the beach, for her way was barred by
shoals that bristled with reefs.

Each wave that struck the coast roared on into the little bays
where it broke on the beach, throwing pebbles fifty feet inland,
then withdrew revealing a great stretch of the sea-bed along the
shore, over which the stones rolled with a hoarse and frightful
noise. Under the lashing of the wind the sea grew rougher by the
moment. The whole channel between this island and the Ile
d'Ambre was one vast sheet of foam deeply furrowed by the dark
troughs of the waves. Along the shore of the bays the foam accumu-
lated in piles more than six feet high from which the sweeping
wind detached innumerable white flakes, carried them up over the
steeply sloping banks, then drove them horizontally more than half
a league inland as far as the foot of the mountains, so that it seemed
as if a snowstorm had blown in from the ocean. The appearance of
the horizon, where the sea was indistinguishable from the sky,
suggested that the tempest would be a long one. Clouds of horrid
shape kept breaking from it and rushing over us with the speed
of birds, whilst others remained high overhead, moving no more
than if they had been great rocks. Not a single patch of blue sky
could be made out in the firmament; only a pallid olive glow lit
every object on the earth, on the sea and in the skies.

The pitching of the vessel soon brought about what we had
dreaded. Her forward lines snapped and with nothing but a single
hawser to hold her, she was driven onto the rocks half a cable's
length from the shore. As if with one voice we all cried out in
distress. Paul was about to fling himself into the sea when I seized
his arm. 'My son,' I said, 'you will surely perish.'

'Let me go and save her,' he cried, 'or let me die.'

Despair had nearly deprived him of his reason. To prevent his loss, Domingue and myself attached a long rope round his waist, keeping hold of the other end. Now swimming, now walking on the reefs, Paul advanced towards the *Saint-Géran*. There were moments when it seemed that he might be able to board her, for the irregular movements of the sea sometimes left the vessel so nearly high and dry that you could have walked round her on foot; but immediately afterwards it would turn about with renewed fury and cover the ship with enormous vaults of water which lifted clear all the forward part of her hull and hurled the unlucky Paul, half-drowned, far up the beach, his chest battered and his legs dripping with blood. As soon as the young man regained the use of his senses, he would get up and make with renewed ardour for the vessel which was fast breaking up under the horrible pounding of the waves. Despairing of saving her, the crew all crowded to the rails and began leaping into the sea on spars, planks, hen-coops, tables and casks.

It was then that we saw an object deserving of eternal pity. A young lady appeared in the stern-gallery of the *Saint-Géran*, stretching forth her arms to him who was making such efforts to reach her. It was Virginia. She had recognized her lover by his fearlessness. The sight of this dear girl exposed to such terrible danger filled us with grief and despair. But Virginia's bearing remained noble and assured, while she waved her hand as if to bid us an eternal farewell. Only one of the sailors had remained on deck, all the others having cast themselves into the sea. He was completely naked and muscular as Hercules. We saw him approach Virginia with respect, throw himself down before her and even do what he could to remove her clothes; but she, turning away her eyes, rejected with dignity his attempts to help her. At once the onlookers redoubled their cries: 'Save her! Save her! Don't leave her!'

But at that very moment a mountain of water of terrifying size swept in between the Ile d'Ambre and the coast and came roaring towards the vessel, its slopes black and its crests foaming. At this dreadful sight the sailor sprang alone into the sea; while Virginia, seeing that death was inevitable, kept one hand on her billowing clothes, placed the other on her heart, and raising upwards eyes shining with serenity, seemed an angel taking flight for heaven.

Alas! O dreadful day! All was swallowed up. A number of the onlookers, whom an impulse of humanity had drawn towards Virginia, were thrown back far up the beach, as was the sailor who had wanted to swim with her to safety. Having escaped from almost certain death, the man knelt down on the sand and said : 'O my God! You have saved my life, but I would have given it willingly for that excellent young lady who would not undress like me.'

Domingue and I drew the unlucky Paul from the water, unconscious and bleeding from the mouth and ears. The governor had him put in the care of some surgeons while we searched along the shore to see whether Virginia's body might not be carried in by the sea; but the wind had suddenly turned about, as it will in a hurricane, and we grieved to think that the unfortunate girl would be denied even the rites of burial. We went away overwhelmed with dismay, each mind struck with a single loss among the great number of souls who had perished in the wreck, and most of us doubting the existence of Providence after witnessing the tragic end of so virtuous a girl; for there are evils so terrible and so undeserved that even the sage finds that his hope is shaken by them.

Paul had meanwhile been taken to one of the neighbouring houses. He was beginning to regain consciousness but was not yet well enough to be carried home. I set off myself with Domingue to prepare Virginia's mother and her friend for news of the disaster. At the entrance to the valley of the Latania River we met some blacks who told us that a lot of debris from the vessel had been washed into the bay opposite. We went down, and almost the first thing I noticed on the shore was Virginia's body. She was half-covered with sand, her head and limbs in the position in which we had seen her perish. Her features had not visibly altered. Her eyes were closed and her face was still serene; but on her cheeks the pale violets of death mingled with the roses of modesty. One of her hands was on her clothes; the other, pressed against her heart, was tightly closed and stiffened. I opened it with difficulty and took from its grasp a little box; but what was my surprise when I saw that it was Paul's portrait, which she had promised him never to part with while she lived. At this final proof of the constancy and love of an unfortunate girl I wept bitterly, while Domingue beat his breast and pierced the air with his cries of grief. We carried Virginia's body to a cabin belonging to some fishermen and left it in the care of a few poor Malabar women who took charge of washing it.

While they were busy with this sad office, we climbed with trembling steps up to the settlement. There we found Madame de la Tour and Marguerite at prayer, waiting for news of the vessel. As soon as she saw me, Madame de la Tour cried out: 'Where is my daughter, my dear daughter, my child?' My silence and my tears leaving her in no doubt of the misfortune that had befallen her, she was at once seized with a painful and suffocating anguish and could utter no other sound than sobs and sighs. For her part Marguerite cried: 'I don't see my son. Where is my son?' and then fainted. We ran to her and, having brought her round, I assured her that Paul was alive and that he was being cared for at the governor's instruction. When she came to herself she thought only of looking after her friend, who kept falling into one long swoon after another. All night long Madame de la Tour was prey to periods of the most cruel suffering, by whose extreme length I was able to judge that no grief is equal to that of a grieving mother. When she did regain consciousness she would turn a fixed and dismal gaze towards heaven. In vain did her friend and I press her hands in ours, in vain did we call her by the most tender names; she appeared to be insensible to these marks of our old affection, and her heavy and laborious breathing was broken only by dull groans.

Early next morning Paul was carried home in a palanquin. He had regained the use of his senses but was unable to utter a word. His meeting with his mother and Madame de la Tour, which at first I had dreaded, brought about more improvement in their condition than anything I had been able to do. A gleam of consolation appeared on the faces of the two unfortunate mothers. Both ran to him, threw their arms around him, kissed him; and the tears which until then had been stifled by the excess of their grief began to flow. Paul soon mixed his own tears with theirs. Nature having thus found relief in these three hapless creatures, a long torpor followed the convulsive stage of their sorrow and procured for them a lethargic repose which in truth resembled the calm of death.

Monsieur de la Bourdonnais sent secretly to inform me that Virginia's body had been carried to the town by his order and that from there it was to be transferred to the church at Pamplemousses. I immediately went down to Port Louis where I found that settlers from every district had gathered for her funeral, as if in her the island had lost its dearest possession. The vessels in the harbour had their yards crossed, their flags at half-mast and were firing their cannon at long intervals. Grenadiers with lowered muskets marched at the head of the procession. Their drums, muffled with black crape, beat only mournful rhythms, and dejection was written on the features of these warriors who had so many times faced death in battle without flinching. Eight young ladies from the most considerable families of the island, dressed in white and carrying palms in their hands, bore the flower-strewn body of their virtuous companion. They were followed by a choir of little children singing hymns. After them came all the most distinguished settlers and officials of the colony, then the governor and last of all a crowd of common people.

Such were the arrangements made by the administration to render some homage to Virginia's virtue. But when her body reached the foot of this mountain, in view of the cabins whose inhabitants she had made happy for so long and whom her death now filled with despair, the whole procession fell into confusion : the hymns and the chanting ceased; only sobbing and sighs of grief rose from the plain. Troops of girls from the neighbouring settlements ran up to touch Virginia's coffin with handkerchiefs, rosaries and crowns of flowers, invoking her as a saint. Mothers asked God for a daughter like her, young men for lovers as constant as she, the poor for a friend as tender-hearted, slaves for so kind a mistress.

When she had been carried to her burial-place, Negresses from Madagascar and Caffres from Mozambique placed baskets of fruit around her and draped pieces of cloth from the trees nearby, according to the custom of their countries; while Indian women from Bengal and the Malabar coast brought cages full of birds which they set free over her body. For the loss of one so deserving of love concerns every nation; and so great is the power of unhappy virtue that all religions are gathered together around its tomb.

Guards had to be posted near her grave to keep back a few girls from poor families who were determined to throw themselves in with Virginia's body, saying that, as they had no further consolation to hope for in this world, all that remained for them was to die with their only benefactress.

She was buried near the church at Pamplemousses, on its western side, beneath a clump of bamboo where, on the way to mass with her mother and Marguerite, she liked to sit and rest beside him she then called her brother.

On his return from the funeral ceremonies Monsieur de la Bourdonnais came up to the settlement, accompanied by a part of his numerous retinue. He offered Madame de la Tour and her friend all the assistance in his power. After briefly expressing his indignation at the conduct of her unnatural aunt, he went to Paul and said everything he could think of to console him. 'I declare before God,' he continued, 'that I acted only for your happiness and that of your family. You must go to France, my friend. I shall obtain a place for you in the king's service, and during your absence I shall care for your mother as if she were my own.' As he spoke he held out his hand, but Paul withdrew his own and turned away his head, unable to look at him.

For myself, I remained at the settlement with my unfortunate friends to give them all the help I could. After three weeks Paul was well enough to walk but his grief seemed to increase as his body regained its strength. He was indifferent to everything; his eyes were lifeless, and none of the questions we put to him could make him reply. Madame de la Tour, who was herself near to death, would often say : 'As long as I see you, my son, I shall seem to see my dear Virginia.' But at the name of Virginia he would shudder and take himself away, despite the urging of his mother who recalled him to her friend's side. Withdrawing alone into the garden, he would sit at the foot of Virginia's coconut-tree and stare at her pool. The governor's surgeon, who had taken the greatest care of him and of the two ladies, told us that to bring him out of his black melancholy we should cross him in nothing but let him do anything he pleased, as there was no other way to overcome his obstinate silence.

I resolved to follow his advice. As soon as Paul felt some small part of his strength return, his first action was to quit the settlement. Determined not to let him out of my sight, I set off after him, telling Domingue to gather some provisions and follow us. The young man's strength and happiness seemed to revive as he went down the mountain. He at once took the road to Pamplemousses; and, when he came to the bamboo-lined walk near the church, proceeded straight to the place where he saw the ground had been freshly turned over : there he knelt down, lifted his eyes to heaven and made a long prayer. This mark of confidence in the Supreme Being was a sign that his soul was beginning to resume its natural operations and seemed to augur well for the return of his reason. Following his example, Domingue and I knelt down and prayed with him. When he had finished, he got up without paying much attention to us and turned his steps towards the north of the island. As I was sure that he knew neither where Virginia's body had been buried nor even whether it had been recovered from the sea, I asked him why he had gone to pray beneath those bamboos. He answered : 'We were so often there.'

He continued on his way as far as the edge of the forest, where night overtook us. There I urged him to follow my example and take some nourishment, after which we lay down to sleep on the grass at the foot of a tree. The next day I thought he would decide to retrace his steps; but although he looked for some time at the church on the plain at Pamplemousses, with its long avenue of bamboos, and even started off as if he meant to return there, he soon plunged abruptly into the forest, still making his way towards the north. I guessed what his purpose was and did my best to turn him from it, but in vain. We reached the Poudre d'Or district towards the middle of the day. He went hurriedly down to the shore at a spot opposite the place where the *Saint-Géran* had been

lost. At the sight of the Ile d'Ambre and its channel, which was
then as calm as a mirror, he cried out: 'Virginia! O my dear Virginia!' and immediately fell into a swoon. Domingue and I carried
him into the forest where we had the greatest difficulty in bringing
him round. As soon as he had regained his senses he wanted to
return to the shore, but when we had begged him not to seek out
those cruel memories which only renewed his sorrow and ours, he
took another direction. In brief, he passed a week re-visiting all the
places he had been with the companion of his childhood. He re-
traced the path she had taken to go and ask pardon for the slave
from the Black River; he returned to the banks of the river of the
Three Paps where she had sat down when unable to walk any
further and the part of the wood where she had lost her way.
Every place that recalled the anxieties, the games, the meals, the
benevolent actions of his beloved – the river of the Long Mountain,
my little house and the waterfall nearby, the papaw-tree she had
planted, the greens where she liked to run, the crossroads in the
forest where she delighted to sing – each in its turn brought him to
tears; and the same echoes which had so many times resounded
with their cries of mutual joy, now sent back only these sorrowful
words: 'Virginia! O my dear Virginia!'

During this wild and vagabond life his eyes became sunken,
his colour turned sallow and his health grew worse and worse. Convinced that our woes are made more acute by the remembrance of
past pleasures and that solitude only increases the passions, I determined to remove my unfortunate friend from the places that kept
the memory of his loss before his mind and to bring him to some
part of the island where he would find plenty of distraction.
Accordingly I led him to a district he had never visited before, the
inhabited heights of the Williams Plains. Here was all the bustle
and variety of agriculture and commerce: gangs of carpenters
squaring timber, others sawing it into planks, wagons and carriages
coming and going along the roads, great herds of cattle and horses
grazing in vast pastures and settlements dotted over the countryside. In several places the elevation of the ground is suitable to
the cultivation of various species of European plants. We saw
corn being harvested on the plain, clearings in the woods carpeted

with strawberry plants and hedges of rose-bushes along the roads. The coolness of the air, by giving tone to the sinews, is even propitious to the health of whites. From these high plains, situated near the middle of the island and surrounded by great woods, neither the sea, nor Port Louis, nor the church at Pamplemousses, nor anything else that might reawaken in Paul the memory of Virginia, could be seen. Even the range of mountains which, on the side of Port Louis, divides into various branches, from the Williams Plains presents to the view only a vertical promontory stretching away in a straight line from which several long pyramids of rocks rise into the gathering clouds.

It was to these plains that I brought Paul. I kept him in constant activity, walking with him day and night, in sunshine and in rain. I purposely led him astray into woods, clearings and fields, aiming to distract his mind by exhausting his body and hoping that these unfamiliar surroundings would divert his thoughts to a different track. But a lover's soul finds traces of its beloved everywhere. Night and day, the calm of solitary places and the noise of settlements, even time itself which effaces so many memories : nothing can separate him from them. In vain do we shake a needle that has been touched by a magnet; no sooner does it come to rest than it turns towards the pole that attracts it. Whenever I asked Paul, as we wandered over the Williams Plains, 'Where shall we go now?' he would turn towards the north and say : 'There are our mountains. Let us return to them.'

I saw at last how fruitless all my attempts to distract him had been. It seemed that the only course remaining to me was to attack his passion directly with all the strength of my poor reason, so I answered : 'Yes, there are the mountains where your dear Virginia lived and here is the portrait you gave her and which, as she was dying, she pressed to a heart still beating for you even at the last.' I held out to him the little portrait he had given Virginia beneath the coconut-trees at the edge of the pool. At the sight of it a baleful joy appeared in his eyes. His weak hands seized it avidly and carried it to his lips. Then his breathing grew laboured and his bloodshot eyes swam with tears that would not flow.

'Listen to me, my son,' I said. 'I am your friend and I was Virginia's. In the midst of your hopes I often tried to fortify your reason against life's unforeseen accidents. What is it that makes you grieve so bitterly now? Is it your own misfortune? Is it Virginia's?

'Your own misfortune is great. There can be no doubt of that. You have lost the dearest of girls, who would have made the most excellent of wives. She had sacrificed her interests to yours and preferred you before fortune, as the only recompense worthy of her virtue. But how can you be sure that the loved one from whom you expected so pure a happiness might not have become instead a source of infinite care? She was disinherited and without possessions. In all your future life you would have had only your labour to share with her. If she had grown more courageous in misfortune, her education had made her more fragile and you would have watched her sinking each day as she did her best to bear a part of your toil. When she had given you children, her cares and yours would have been increased by the difficulties of providing between you for aged parents and a growing family.

' "The governor would have helped us," you will say. But in a colony where the officials change so often, how do you know that you would always have had men like Monsieur de la Bourdonnais? That you would never have been sent wicked and unprincipled governors? That your wife might not have been obliged to curry favour with them to obtain some paltry relief? Either she would have been weak and you much to be pitied, or she would have been honourable and you would have remained poor – and been fortunate if her beauty and virtue did not earn you the persecution of the very men whose protection you had hoped for.

' "There would still have remained," you will say, "the happiness, independent of fortune, that consists in protecting the object of our love which, the weaker it is, the more it attaches itself to us. I could have consoled Virginia with my own anxieties, made her rejoice in my sadness and increased our love by our shared affliction." No doubt virtue and love do enjoy these bitter pleasures. But she is no more, and you are left with those that she loved most after you, her mother and yours, whom you will bring to the grave if you persist in this inconsolable grief. Make it your happiness to help them as she made it hers. Beneficence, my son, is the happiness of virtue. No other on earth is greater or more assured. It is not for man, weak and fleeting traveller that he is, to form projects of pleasure and delight, repose, abundance and glory. You see how one step towards the acquisition of fortune has hurled us all from abyss to abyss. True, you were opposed to it, but who would have doubted that Virginia's voyage was to end in her happiness and yours? The invitations of an aged and wealthy relation, the advice of a judicious governor, the approbation of an entire colony, the exhortation and authority of a priest – these decided Virginia's fate. Thus do we rush to our ruin, deceived by the very prudence of those in authority over us. It would no doubt have been better not to have believed them, not to have listened to the voice of a deceiving world or put faith in its expectations. And yet, look at all the men going about their business on these plains and think of all those others who go to India in search of fortune or of those who calmly reap the benefits of their labour without stirring from their houses in Europe; which of them is not destined one day to lose what he cherishes most : honours, fortune, wife, children, friends? To the memory of their loss most of them will add that of their own imprudence. Not so you : examine your conscience and you will find no cause for self-reproach. You kept your faith. In the flower of youth you had the prudence of a sage because you never strayed from what you felt was true to Nature. Your views alone were just because they were pure, simple and disinterested; and because no fortune could weigh against your sacred claims to Virginia's affection. You have lost her, but it was not imprudence or greed or worldly wisdom that caused your loss. God himself employed the passions of others to remove the object of your love; God, the giver of all you possess, who knows what is most fitting for you, and whose wisdom has not left you any cause for the repentance and despair that follow on the heels of the evils that we bring upon ourselves.

'In your adversity you can say to yourself : "It was not of my making." Is it then Virginia's misfortune, her end, her present condition that give you cause to grieve? She has suffered the fate reserved for birth, for beauty, for empires themselves. The life of man, with all its plans, is but a little tower capped by death. The moment she was born she was condemned to die. It was her good fortune to have loosened the ties of life before her mother, before yours, before you and thus to be spared the necessity of dying several deaths before the last one.

'Death is a blessing for all men, my son. It is the night of this unquiet day which we call life. In the sleep of death the sickness and pain, the griefs and fears with which we unhappy mortals are ceaselessly troubled are stilled forever. Look closely at those men who appear most fortunate and you will see that their so-called happiness has been bought very dearly : public esteem by domestic strife, riches by loss of health, the rare pleasure of being loved by continual sacrifices; and after an existence devoted to others' interests they often find themselves surrounded only by false friends and ungrateful relations. But Virginia was happy to the very last. The blessings of Nature made her so when she was with us and those of virtue when she was far away; and even in that terrible moment when we saw her perish, she was happy still. For, whether she cast her eyes upon the universal desolation that she caused in an entire colony or upon you who flew so fearlessly to her aid, she saw how dear she was to us all. She found strength for what was to come by recalling the innocence of her life and was granted the reward that Heaven reserves for virtue, a courage greater than her danger. She faced death with a serene countenance.

'My son, God makes virtue suffer every accident of human existence, to show that it alone can turn them to good use and find happiness and glory in so doing. When He has marked it out for an illustrious reputation, He raises it upon a great stage and sets it to struggle with death. In this way its courage serves as an example and the memory of its misfortune receives a tribute of tears from posterity for ever. Such is the immortal monument which is set apart for virtue in a world where everything passes away and where even the memory of most kings is soon swallowed up in eternal oblivion.

'But Virginia has not ceased to exist. You see, my son, on earth everything changes but nothing is lost. To annihilate even the smallest particle of matter is beyond the art of man. Then how can what was capable of reason, feeling, love, virtue and religion have perished when the elements that clothed it are indestructible? Ah! if Virginia was happy with us, she is much happier now. There is a God, my son: all Nature proclaims it, I have no need to prove it to you. Only the wickedness of men makes them deny a divine justice which they fear. You feel His existence in your heart just as you see His works before your eyes. And do you think that He has left Virginia without reward? Do you think that the same power which could clothe so noble a soul in a form so lovely that you sensed God's handiwork in it, could not snatch her from the waves? That He who has contrived the present happiness of men by laws that are unknown to you could not prepare another happiness for Virginia by laws equally unknown? Before we came into being, if we had been capable of thought, could we have formed an idea of our own existence to come? And now that we are in this shadowy and fleeting existence can we foresee what lies beyond the death by which we must leave it? Has God a need, like man, to make this little globe of earth the theatre for His intelligence and goodness? Could He not have made human life grow elsewhere than in these fields of death? There is not a single drop of water in the ocean that is not full of living creatures which are our concern, and is there nothing for us among the myriad stars that revolve above our heads? What! Is there no supreme intelligence, no divine goodness, except in the place where we find ourselves? And in those innumerable radiant globes, in the infinite fields of light that surround them, which neither night nor storm ever darkens, is there only empty space and eternal nothingness? If we, who owe nothing we have to ourselves, dared assign bounds to the Power that has given us everything, might we not imagine ourselves here as at the limits of His empire, where life struggles with death and innocence with tyranny?

'There can be no doubt that somewhere there is a place where virtue receives its reward and where Virginia is now happy. Ah! if from the abode of the angels she could open her heart to you, she would say as she did when she bade you goodbye: "Oh Paul! life is but a trial. I have been found faithful to the laws of Nature, of love and of virtue. I crossed the seas in obedience to my family; I gave up riches to keep faith with you, and I preferred to lose my life rather than violate modesty. Heaven found that enough of my earthly course had been run. From poverty, calumny, tempests and the spectacle of others' woes I am safe forever. I am beyond the reach of all the evils that men fear – and you pity me! I am pure and unalterable as a particle of light – and you recall me to life's darkness! Oh Paul! Oh my dear friend! Do you remember those days of happiness when from early morning we drank in the delights of the skies, rising with the sun as it touched the peaks of our rocks and streaming with its rays through the depths of our forests? We experienced a rapture whose cause was beyond our comprehension. In our innocent desires we wished to be all sight to enjoy the rich colours of the dawn, all smell to breathe the perfume of our plants, all hearing to listen to the concerts of our birds, and all heart to be grateful for these blessings. Now, at the fountain-head of beauty, whence flows all that gives pleasure on earth, my soul sees, tastes, hears, and touches directly what then it perceived only through the dull organs of sense. Ah! how can tongue describe the eternal orient shores where now I dwell forever? All that infinite power and heavenly goodness can create to console an unfortunate creature, all the harmony of raptures shared in friendship by an infinite number of beings rejoicing in the same felicity, we experience unalloyed. Be steadfast in the trial that is given to you so that you may increase your Virginia's happiness by a love that will have no end and nuptials whose torches can never be extinguished. Then will I assuage your longing, then will I wipe away your tears. Oh my dear friend! my young husband! lift up your soul towards the infinite, to help you bear the troubles of a moment." '

My own emotion had put an end to my discourse when Paul cried out, his eyes fixed upon me : 'She is gone. She is gone.' Having pronounced these doleful words he fell into a long swoon. When he came to himself, he said : 'Since death is a blessing and Virginia is happy, I wish to die too, so that I can be with her again.' My efforts at consolation had only added fuel to his despair. I was like a man attempting to save a friend who refuses to swim even though he is sinking in the midst of a river. Grief had overwhelmed him.

Alas! the pains of childhood prepare a man to enter life and Paul had never experienced them.

I brought him back to the settlement. There I found his mother and Madame de la Tour in a state of languishment which had worsened in our absence. Marguerite seemed to be the more downcast. The lively nature, on which slight troubles make no impression, is the one that offers least resistance to great sorrows.

'Oh my good neighbour,' she said, 'last night I thought I saw Virginia clothed all in white and standing amidst delectable groves and gardens. "The happiness I enjoy is worthy to be envied," she told me. Then she drew near to Paul with a joyful air and carried him away with her. As I strove to hold him back, I felt that I too was leaving the earth, following my son with inexpressible delight. I wanted to bid my friend goodbye : at once I saw that she was following us with Marie and Domingue. But what I find stranger still is that Madame de la Tour also had a dream last night which included the same details.'

'My friend,' I replied, 'I believe that nothing happens in the world without God's permission. Dreams sometimes prefigure the truth.'

Madame de la Tour recounted a dream similar in every point to her friend's. As I had never noticed in either lady any tendency to superstition, I was struck by the concordance of their dreams; and there was no doubt in my mind that what they foretold would come about. The belief that truth is sometimes revealed to us during sleep is found among all the peoples of the earth. It was credited by the greatest of the ancients, among them Alexander, Caesar, the Scipios, the two Catos and Brutus, none of whom were men of feeble intellect. The Old and the New Testaments provide numerous examples of dreams that have come true. For my part, I have only to consult my own experience in the matter; more than once I have found that dreams are warnings given by some superior intelligence concerned with our welfare. It is impossible to advance arguments for and against things that are beyond the light of human reason. However, man's reason is but a reflection of God's; and since we know that man has the power to make his intentions manifest at the ends of the earth by hidden and secret means, why should not the intelligence that governs the universe use similar means for the same purpose? A friend can console a friend by a letter which crosses a multitude of kingdoms, passes amidst the hatred of nations and arrives bringing hope and joy to one man; cannot the Sovereign Protector of Innocence find some secret way to send assistance to a virtuous soul which puts its confidence in Him alone? What need has He to employ visible means to carry out His will, He who proceeds in all His works by unceasing spiritual influence?

Why should we doubt the truth of dreams? What is life itself, with all its vain and fleeting projects, if not a dream?

At all events, what my unfortunate friends had dreamed soon came to pass. Paul died two months after the death of his beloved Virginia, whose name had never left his lips. A week after her son's end, Marguerite greeted her own with a joy that only virtue can experience. She took a most tender leave of Madame de la Tour, 'in the expectation,' she said, 'of a sweet and everlasting reunion. We should desire death as the greatest of blessings,' she added. 'If life is a punishment, we must wish it to end; if it is a trial, we must ask that it be short.'

The government provided for Marie and Domingue, who were no longer able to work and who did not long survive their mistresses. As for poor Fidele, he had pined away and died about the same time as his master.

I brought Madame de la Tour to my settlement. In the midst of such heavy losses she had borne up with a greatness of soul that was beyond belief, consoling Paul and Marguerite to the last as if she had no misfortune to endure but theirs. Even when they were no longer to be seen she spoke of them to me every day as of dearly loved friends who lived nearby. Yet she survived them no more than a month. Far from reproaching her aunt for the harm she had done, she prayed to God to pardon her and to allay the anguish of mind into which, we learned, she had fallen immediately after sending Virginia so heartlessly away.

That unnatural woman did not suffer the punishment of her harshness for very long. From several vessels which arrived in succession I learned that she was much troubled with the vapours, which rendered life and death equally intolerable. Sometimes she blamed herself for the premature end of her charming grand-niece and the loss of her mother which it had caused; while at other times she congratulated herself for having thrust far from her two wretched creatures whose base inclinations had dishonoured her family. She would fly into a rage at the sight of the great number of miserable poor who crowd the streets of Paris. 'Why are these idlers not sent to perish in our colonies?' she would cry, adding that the notions of humanity, virtue and religion common to all peoples had only been invented by their princes as instruments of policy. Then, flying suddenly to the opposite extreme, she would give way to superstitious terrors which filled her with mortal dread. She would rush to the rich monks who were her spiritual directors, bringing alms in great quantity and begging them to appease the Divinity by the sacrifice of her fortune, as if what she had refused to those in distress could please the Father of Mankind. Often she fancied that she saw fiery plains and burning mountains, where hideous spectres roamed howling her name. Then she would throw herself at the feet of her directors, imagining the tortures and the torments she would have to suffer; for Heaven, just Heaven, sends a fearful religion to cruel souls.

She went on like this for several years, by turns atheistical and superstitious, holding life and death in equal abhorrence. But what finally put an end to so deplorable an existence was the very thing to which she had sacrificed her natural feelings. She learned with great vexation that after her death her fortune would be inherited by some relations whom she detested. To prevent this happening she tried to dispose of the greater part of it while she could, but her relations were able, on account of her persistent attacks of vapours, to have her confined as insane and her estate put in the hands of a trustee. Thus it was that her riches sealed her ruin; and as they had hardened the heart of her who possessed them, so did they pervert the hearts of those who hankered after them. At last she died; and, as if to cap her misfortune, she retained sufficient use of her reason to realize that she was dispossessed and despised by the very persons by whose opinion she had been governed throughout life.

Paul was laid to rest under the bamboos near his friend Virginia. Their loving mothers and their faithful servants were placed around them. No marble was raised over their humble mounds, no inscription was cut to their virtues, but their memory has remained indelible in the hearts of those who experienced their kindness. Their shades have no need of the celebrity that they shunned in life; but if they concern themselves still with what happens on earth, no doubt they choose to wander beneath the thatched roofs that shelter laborious virtue, to console poverty unhappy with its lot and to nurture in young lovers a lasting flame, a taste for Nature's gifts, a love of work and a dread of riches.

The voice of the people, which says nothing of the monuments raised to the glory of kings, has given names to some parts of this island which will perpetuate the memory of Virginia's loss. Amidst the reefs near the Ile d'Ambre you can see a place called 'The Saint-Géran Channel', from the name of the vessel that was lost there as it brought her back from Europe. The tip of that long point of land which you can see at a distance of three leagues from here, half-submerged by the waves, and which the *Saint-Géran* was unable to get round the day before the hurricane to enter the harbour, is called the 'Cape of Misfortune'; and here before us, at the end of the valley, is 'Tomb Bay', where we found Virginia buried in the sand, as if the sea had wished to return her body to her family and render a last homage to her modesty on those same shores she had honoured with her innocence.

Young people so tenderly united! unfortunate mothers! dear family! these woods that gave you shade, these fountains that flowed for you, these hills where you took your repose together, still lament your loss. None after you has dared to till this desolate ground or rebuild these humble cabins. Your goats have run wild, your orchards are destroyed, your birds have fled; nothing can be heard but the cries of the sparrow-hawks as they circle high above this rocky valley. As for myself, since I looked upon you for the last time I have been like a friend bereft of friends, like a father who has lost his children, like a traveller left to wander over the earth alone.

As he spoke these words the good old man went away shedding

tears, and my own had fallen more than once in the course of his melancholy narration.

NOTES

PAGE 37   This Preface was composed for the first appearance in print
of *Paul and Virginia* in the 4th volume of the 3rd edition of
the author's *Studies of Nature* (1788). It was accompanied in
the first separate edition (1789) by a Foreword; in the
edition of 1806 both were replaced by a long Preamble.

Theocrituses and Virgils: types of the pastoral poet of antiquity. Theocritus was a Greek poet of the third century
BC, among whose works are a number of pastoral poems.
Virgil's *Georgics* and some of his *Eclogues* treat rural subjects and themes.

Ile de France: the novel is set on this island of volcanic formation which lies in the Indian Ocean some five hundred
miles east of Madagascar. It was given the name Mauritius
by the Dutch who took possession in 1598. The French held
it from 1715-1810 and called it the Ile de France. The
British captured it in 1810, restored the name Mauritius and
kept possession until independence in 1968. The island is
38 miles long and 26 miles wide.

44   *Yolof Negro*: one of a Negro people from Senegal, West
Africa.

pagnes: a pagne is a piece of material woven from strands
of bark or grass and used for clothing, especially as a loin-
cloth.

46   *the constellation Gemini*: 'The Twins', or Castor and
Pollux, were born from an egg after their mother Leda had
been impregnated by Jupiter in the form of a swan. They
were set among the heavens as a reward for their brotherly
love. Helen of Troy was their sister and was born from the
same conception.

47   *children of Leda*: see previous note. In some versions of
the story it is Helen and Polydeuces (Pollux) who are children of Zeus (Jupiter) and born from the same egg.

Creoles: a person of European stock born in a French colony
is usually meant by the word; less frequently a Negro born
in a colony rather than brought from Africa.

48   *Niobe's children*: Niobe, daughter of Tantalus and wife of Amphion, ruler of Thebes, boasted of her divine ancestry and her seven sons and seven daughters, exalting herself above the goddess Leto who had only two children, Apollo and Diana. The goddess sent hers to slay Niobe's with arrows. Niobe herself was transformed into a statue which continued to shed tears of grief.

    Monsieur de la Bourdonnais: Bertrand François Mahé, Comte de la Bourdonnais (1699-1753), governor-general of the French Mascarenes from 1735-1746. He established the seat of his government on the Ile de France, encouraged the commercial development of the island and built a naval base at Port Louis.

52   *five leagues*: one league is approximately three miles.

    The bread of the wicked: based on Proverbs 20:17: 'Bread of deceit is sweet to a man; but afterwards his mouth shall be filled with gravel.' Madame de la Tour's version lays characteristic stress on virtuous independence.

54   *The Three Paps*: 'There are many mountains whose summits are rounded in the shape of breasts and which are so called in all languages. They are in fact true breasts for from them flow many of the rivers and streams that spread plenty over the earth. The greatest of the rivers that supply it with water have their sources in such mountains where they are constantly furnished with moisture from the clouds that gather ceaselessly round the peaks of rock that rise up from their centres like nipples. These admirable instances of Nature's providence have been pointed out in the preceding *Studies*' (Bernardin's note).

    ajoupa: a shelter made by covering stakes with branches and leaves.

56   *take your scent from them*: 'This astute action of Domingue and his dog Fidele closely resembles that of the savage Tewenissa and his dog Oniah, as reported by Monsieur de Crèvecoeur in a book full of humanity: *Letters from an American Planter*' (Bernardin's note).

61   *Fratres Helenae* .... : Horace, *Odes* I:3. Horace's poem is a prayer for the safe completion of his friend Virgil's ocean voyage, as well as a warning against overstepping divinely-set limits, in particular sailing the dangerous sea. Helen's brothers are Castor and Pollux (see notes to pp. 46-7), the twins of the constellation Gemini and traditional protectors of seamen.

    Fortunatus et ille ... : Virgil, *Georgics* II:493.

62   *At secura quies* .... : Virgil, *Georgics* II:467.

65   *palanquins*: litters fitted with a bamboo pole and carried by slaves.

67   *the shepherds of Midian*: Exodus 2:15-21.

       the unfortunate Ruth: actually Ruth, a Moabitess, returns not to her own home but to Bethlehem, the home of her deceased husband and of her mother-in-law Naomi.

69   *cassava roots*: cassava (*manihot utilissima*) is a shrub with fleshy edible roots which, grated and made into cakes, formed the staple diet of slaves on the island.

70   *fauns and dryads*: fauns: minor deities of woodland and countryside; dryads: tree-nymphs; the life of each was bound to that of a particular tree and ended when the tree died.

73   *Caffre*: a Negro from south-east Africa belonging to the Bantu family. The word, from the Arabic *kafir* (infidel), was originally applied to those peoples which had not embraced Islam.

75   *Saint Paul*: Paul of Thebes (died *c.*340), an early, and traditionally the first, Christian hermit. He is said to have escaped the persecution of Decius by fleeing to a cave near the Red Sea where he lived for about ninety years supplying himself with food and drink from a nearby palm-tree and spring and fashioning the palms into a tunic for clothing.

79   *piastres*: silver coins of wide currency and varying value.

88   *Ile Bourbon*: the island of Réunion, a French possession since 1638.

91   *Telemachus*: the didactic novel *Télémaque* (1699) was written for the instruction of the grandson of Louis XIV, the young Duke of Burgundy, by his tutor the Abbé Fénelon. It recounts the adventures of Telemachus in search of his father Ulysses and includes much moral and political reflection.

       Antiope: the daughter of King Idomeneus; she is loved by Telemachus and destined to become his wife.

       Eucharis: one of the nymphs on Calypso's island; Telemachus is rescued from her charms by Mentor.

102   *Corps*: privileged bodies of those holding office by royal appointment in the various branches (judiciary, military, etc.) of the public service.

113   *Xenophon*: In his *Anabasis*, Xenophon relates how he accompanied a force of 10,000 Greek soldiers in the service of the younger Cyrus in an expedition against the latter's brother Artaxerxes II of Persia. After the death of Cyrus and the execution of the Greek generals, Xenophon was largely responsible for the successful return journey of the Greek

contingent. He later served the Spartan King Agesilaus and, exiled from Athens, spent the next twenty years on a country estate in Sparta hunting and composing his numerous literary works.

Scipio Africanus: Publius Cornelius Scipio (236-*c*.183 BC, known as Africanus Major), the victor in the battle of Zama in the Second Punic War, was later accused of taking bribes and misuse of public funds and, although not found guilty, withdrew to his estate at Liternum. He was an enthusiastic student of Greek culture. Publius Cornelius Scipio Aemilianus (*c*.185-129 BC, known as Africanus Minor), who destroyed Carthage in 146 at the end of the Third Punic War, was an orator and patron of Greek and Latin Literature. Either may be intended, though the elder seems the more likely.

Lucullus: a Roman general and statesman of the first century BC (*c*.114-57). He conducted a series of successful military campaigns but lost his command and thereafter devoted himself to his luxurious tastes and his passion for Greek literature of which he possessed an extensive library.

Catinat: Nicolas Catinat (1637-1712) was made a Marshal of France by Louis XIV in 1693. He was not on good terms with the court and after his defeat at Carpi during the war of the Spanish succession he retired in disgrace.

the Hours . . . horses of the sun: In Greek mythology the Hours were goddesses of the seasons. Ovid (*Metamorphoses* II:116-121) imagines them as yoking the horses that pulled the Sun's chariot and leading them from their stables.

114   *24 December, 1744 . . . Saint Géran . . . Monsieur Aubin*: The actual *Saint-Géran* broke up on the reefs near the Ile d'Ambre and sank on 17 August, 1744. The captain's name was Monsieur Delamare. Bernardin transposes the shipwreck to the hurricane season and has it take place on Christmas Day.

118   *bower-cable*: a cable attached to one of the anchors (best bower and small bower) carried at the bows of a vessel.

119   *taffrail*: 'the aftermost portion of the poop-rail of a ship' (*OED*).

122   *Malabar women*: from the Malabar Coast in south-west India.

126   *Williams Plains*: high plains in the south-west portion of the centre of the island.

133   *the greatest of the ancients*: for the Scipios see note to page 113. The two Catos were Marcus Porcius Cato (234-149 BC, known as Censorius) and his great-grandson Marcus Porcius

Cato (95-46 BC, known as Uticensis). Brutus was the conspirator Marcus Junius Brutus (78?-42 BC).

134   *the vapours*: in older medical usage a nervous condition, especially hysteria, hypochondria and depression of spirits, attributed to the morbid effects of exhalations developed within the lower organs (stomach, spleen, liver, etc.) and rising to the brain.